T0284708

HOWARD AKLER

SPLITS VILLE

Coach House Books | Toronto

copyright © Howard Akler, 2018

first edition

Published with the generous assistance of the Canada Council for the
Arts and the Ontario Arts Council. Coach House Books also acknowl-
edges the support of the Government of Canada through the Canada
Book Fund and the Government of Ontario through the Ontario Book
Publishing Tax Credit.

*Please note that this is a work of fiction. While some events and characters are
rooted in historical fact, this is a fictional interpretation of that history.*

LIBRARY AND ARCHIVES CANADA CATALOGUING IN PUBLICATION

Akler, Howard, 1969-, author
        Splitsville / Howard Akler.

 Issued in print and electronic formats.
ISBN 978-1-55245-373-5 (softcover).

        I. Title.

PS8601.K56S65 2018   c813'.6   C2018-903943-4
                                                          C2018-903944-2

Splitsville is available as an ebook: ISBN 978 1 77056 567 8 (EPUB), ISBN
978 1 77056 568 5 (PDF)

Purchase of the print version of this book entitles you to a free digital
copy. To claim your ebook of this title, please email sales@chbooks.com
with proof of purchase. (Coach House Books reserves the right to terminate
the free digital download offer at any time.)

for Hazel Akler

PART ONE

Sachs unpacks. His hands vanish inside a carton and come out with a pair of old books. He blows the dust off their covers. Glances briefly at condition and title, then begins a pile on his left. He pulls out another, a thick one. Hefts it. Runs his forefinger along deckled pages and adds it to the other two. The stack grows – slipcased, hardcovered, spine-cracked. Lily watches without impatience, oddly absorbed by his silent assessments. She shifts her weight. The floor creaks. Sachs looks up, purses his lips as if to speak, but in the end he says nothing.

This is how you always imagine him. This moment: in a thin cardigan, with a thick Adam's apple. Stack of books on his desk, a dozen more on the floor. Stacks and stacks with clear precipitous balance. He and Lily are alone in the shop. He thumbs a recto, the pages suddenly so cathected that when she brushes a strand of hair behind her ear the act becomes indecent.

Theirs was a lingering fling. Six months all told, January to June, 1971. Not even a flicker in history and yet something in the nature of ardour emanates still, forty-five years later.

◊

The old bookshop has been vacant for years. It was a pho joint for a stretch, a printer's prior to that. You study grime on the display window. Peer past. It's an abject fenestration. The fixtures remain the same, tiles on the floor perhaps also. What else? You lock your bike in the late morning sun. Squint streetwise. This was the city that saved nothing, that for decades did little but demolish and rebuild. The rarity of Spadina Avenue is its bric-a-brac evolution: twentieth-century storefronts nailed onto nineteenth-century mansions, Chinese street signs with the names of dead British statesmen: Cecil, Baldwin, D'Arcy. You step back, the capacious sidewalk suddenly stuffed with eyes.

A ramshackle gent steps off the curb in sync with a gangly kid in a hoodie. You follow, between fenders and then the first three lanes of traffic. Watch a streetcar glide south, a trio of jaywalkers who make way. Everyone hustles to the safety of the sidewalks. You huff between a tattoo parlour and a board-game café, turn onto Oxford, and there, before a row of mephitic Victorians, you arrive at last at a single diastolic moment. You text Es quick dumb endearments. She's due any day, enormous, unable to do much except watch nature documentaries on Netflix and wait for the next appointment with the midwife. Not you. You, with a crib still to assemble, accepted her entreaty and got out of the apartment.

You jostle and are jostled. Make your way past a new tacqueria, dives real and faux. The clenched streets of Kensington Market. Oxford and Augusta are dense with transaction. You dodge a delivery truck, three cyclists, and a dog and end up at one of your old haunts, a post-and-beam place with a Hindu barista and distressed tables. You sit down with your demitasse. You never take sugar, but you like to twiddle the spoon.

◊

It begins with a death. One of his regulars, Sid Klein, who liked books about tough Jews and who was himself tough enough not to squawk during a deep December chill on the picket line. He was an organizer, a diehard. Barely even flinched before pneumonia did him in on New Year's Eve.

Sachs is more of a slouch. He skips the sub-zero graveside service and shows up in the Sullivan Street apartment for the shiva. Mourners elbow-to-elbow. Distant Klein cousins lurch for the coffee cake, distraught needleworkers pass a flask. Sachs shuffles through, and there, among the stooped and the bulbous, comes sudden terrible knowledge: all his best customers are dying off.

He loosens his tie, looks both ways for the daughter, a high school civics teacher. He offers his condolences.

I'm a little relieved actually, says Lily Klein. It would've been just like him to drag it out.

She sloshes her glass. That sounds terrible, doesn't it?

Sachs shrugs. It's a difficult time.

Plus, I've been drinking too much.

Plus, maybe you've been drinking too much.

He sees her pupils dilate; in the wider aperture perhaps some shifting appraisal. None of their previous conversations were personal – he would pull a book off the shelf for her, point out something on the spinner rack. But now she leans close. She smells of whisky and oranges.

We've been packing up his books, she says.

Bring them by, he says. I can have a look.

She nods. Make me an offer.

Their talk mingles with the mourner's prayer. Ten men in solemn recitation. Sachs an unbeliever, but something nonetheless begins to stir. He has a boner at the Kaddish.

◊

How quickly the past scrolls by. Pages and pages of old newspaper on your phone, months of digitized broadsheet passing so rapidly your eyes are soon stuffed with a faded quotidian: bell-bottoms on sale at Simpsons, ten-cent cups of coffee. You sit here, sip your three-dollar espresso, and zoom in on decades-old coverage of the failed Spadina Expressway. You read items about appropriated homes, air pollution. Uptown and downtown rhetoric. In concrete terms, Spadina was to be six miles of six-lane road. Citizens of the mid-century were told to look forward to speedy trips through town, the flow of traffic from home to work and back would be unimpeded by stoplights and occluded streets. The old future was sleek, antiseptic, fast. Or so the planners said. The future that actually arrived was far messier.

◊

Cecil Street Books. The sign reads: *Used and Rare.* Through the big store window, a subdued January light falls on photos of Paley and Koufax and also the back of Hal Sachs. He lugs an armful of poetry. Jams a Mandelstam.

Lily shows up with a cabload of cartons. Sachs begins to examine her father's library. There's an Arendt, of course, and one or two by Nizer. Gentle foxing on the Liebling. Worn paperbacks by Appel and Gold and then a real find: Helstein's 1929 translation of *Red Cavalry* – the first in English – but with comments, alas, in the dead man's hand.

Marginalia, says Sachs.

He always said he couldn't think without a pencil in his hand.

Don't much care for other people's scribbles. It's like trying to watch a movie with someone nattering in your ear.

Lily smiles without humour. He was a natterer all right.

Sachs rolls up the sleeves of his denim shirt. He has thin forearms, dusty fingernails. He shoots a brief grey squint at his surroundings: three aisles in the shop run the same way for two generations. A lineage bookish and commodified. The original proprietors, his parents, sniffed out Spadina opportunity and for years cajoled a living out of the same spot. Their renown ran for blocks, their scion wracked with constancy.

Lily returns two days later with a last box. She sees Sachs twiddle his pencil, his elbow abutting *Books in Print*. She takes a step closer but his eyes remain far-off.

What're you thinking about?

About getting a cup of coffee. Join me?

Down Spadina they go, light flurries on lintel and dormer. They pass a three-store complex with two vacancies and the holdout, Kaplan Imports, about to bite the dust. They watch the missus paper over the window.

Lily blows on her hands. Fucking expressway, she says. It's going to kill this street.

Sachs shrugs. There's still time, he says. Nothing's been decided.

All the big money's behind it. That's the real problem. Capital has become consolidated into fewer and fewer hands.

They cross the street to Switzer's. Sachs holds the door open and smiles. I'm buying, he says.

◊

This is a story about growth, about a city that doubled in size. From the 1950s to the 1970s, two decades, more than a million newcomers: Hungarians, Vietnamese, Koreans, Portuguese. The old downtown neighbourhoods and streets no longer fit. Borders were loosened, an uneasy alliance nego-tiated between the urban centre and surrounding villages, townships. The suburban sprawl called for order and control, so a new tier of administrators – Metro – was set up to coordinate massive new infrastructure projects: water mains, sewer systems, the first subway line, a series of expressways. Fred C. Gardiner, former reeve of Forest Hill village, was in charge. They called him Big Daddy.

◊

Nothing but browsers when he returns. Mrs. Mintz at the spinner rack, a young couple cooing in History. Sachs at his desk does some foot dangling and, after long internal debate, gets off his duff. He continues to straighten Poetry, eyeballs the distance between spines and then stuffs in another. This is the most limited of muscle memory – schlep and shelve – the familiar task that frees up enough space for any meagre detail to hit with concussive, useless force.

My nerves are strained, he locates in a Yevtushenko, *like wires between the city of No and the city of Yes!*

He inspects Crane's *Collected Stories*. Nice tight spine, small stain on the flyleaf. Next, a pristine copy of *The Double Hook*. He prices them in pencil, the lulling scratch of graphite silenced by sudden horripilation. He rates a Berenice Abbott monograph without scrutiny, then an illustrated *Bartleby* he fingers like a bruise.

◊

You were three years old when your uncle disappeared. The news has lingered in your ears almost half a century and now echoes, because of your soon-to-be-born child, with fresh inflection. The due date is June 2, which also happens to be the last day Hal Sachs was ever seen.

There was no note. The police asked their obligatory questions, but answers only came later, with a slight shift of emphasis. He went from *missing* to *gone*. Four letters filled with a wrong-eared finality; unlike the permanance of death or divorce, a man who disappears can still return.

There was always something so damned equivocal about the man, Lily Klein told you years later.

◊

Metro's plan was ambitious: a series of wider, faster roads that would connect the old with the new. Spadina was only the start; once completed, it would be hitched up to future inner-city routes, like the Crosstown and the Christie-Clinton. The whole thing was mapped out decades in advance. Sam Cass, the roads and traffic commissioner, wanted every Torontonian to be no more than three-quarters of a mile from the nearest on-ramp.

Earlier expressways ran along natural corridors, Don River to the east and Lake Ontario to the south, and so caused relatively little disruption. Not so Spadina. Plans called for it to rumble right through the heart of the city. Houses in middle-class neighbourhoods such as Cedarvale and the Annex would be appropriated and demolished. Buildings would be razed, then paved over for parking lots. Outraged residents found their collective voice and shouted STOP. Many uptowners, those desperate for an unfettered route downtown, had an equally loud retort: GO.

It was a war of words.

The Spadina Expressway was to be built in segments. When the initial two-mile stretch from Wilson Heights south to Lawrence Avenue was completed in 1967, the GO side was giddy. Their city was taking shape. No less pleased were the owners of the new Yorkdale Shopping Plaza – vehicles off-ramped right to their front doors. The department-store lobby was adamant things continue apace.

So, on it went. Land from Lawrence down to Eglinton Avenue was cleared. A ditch was dug. The roadbed was completed but not yet paved before opposition grew too loud for politicians to ignore. They halted construction and referred the matter to the body of provincial oversight, the Ontario Municipal Board, for review. For the next eighteen months, everyone idled.

◊

Lily comes back from bereavement leave and discovers her Grade 11 class at Harbord Collegiate to be clobbered by ennui. The substitute teacher took two days to describe the passage of a private member's bill in the provincial legislature, a detailed incursion of gobbledygook that levelled the kids' already unsteady attention spans. So, the first thing Lily has to do is prod them, revive their interest in civics with the lingo of resistance. She steers the lecture toward the Spadina Expressway battle, even manages to use the phrase *Stick it to the man* with a straight face.

First they said it'd cost thirty million, Lily says. Then seventy million. Now it's two hundred million. Maybe more. For a road. A big road, mind you. An expressway that will run six lanes from Wilson down to Dupont. McLuhan says it'll be like a dagger through the heart of the city.

Who? says Jerry, from the front row. A furious note-taker, he fumbles with his eraser.

The point is: people are really steamed. They're organizing. That's the true meaning of democracy. It's not as simple as majority rules. It's more about voice, about speaking up and about the city learning to listen to other points of view.

She wears a snug navy blouse. There's a loose thread on her suede skirt. Lily just beyond thirty though surely ante-diluvian in the eyes of her students.

Remember, guys, political power is no longer relegated to the voting booth. That's what the STOP movement is all about. Thoughts?

So many gazes go deskbound. The jocks and heads, of course, but also the browners too preoccupied by insistent intense feelings and resultant vague notions. Their adulthood coming both too fast and not fast enough.

Yes, Trudy?

Will this be on the test?

The period ticks down. She spots Principal Libov at the door. With his flat head squashed onto his shoulders, he looks like a man perpetually ducking for cover.

Lillian? he says. A word.

She's a good two inches taller than the principal, but opts for subtler advantage. Sits on the edge of the desk so her eyes, while resolute, remain level with his.

Lillian, says Libov.

He offers the weakest smile she's ever seen.

No one is happier to see you back than I. Really. Your enthusiasm for the subject matter is, uh, admirable, especially after your leave of absence. Our students have always responded well to you.

But?

But.

Libov strides to the chalkboard. He grabs a piece of chalk and crosses out her squiggled definitions of gradual and cataclysmic money. His Xs are quite firm.

We've discussed this before. Your personal opinions are not part of the curriculum.

Can't you please cut me some slack, Marv?

Libov sighs. Look, he says. You have only recently suffered a grievous loss. I understand. Your judgment is askew. Let me straighten it out for you. No more straying from the material. No more tangents. Capisce?

Lily looks down at the textbook. She drums her fingers.

Car horns collide at an advanced green. Two storeys up, a window rattles in the frame. Their apartment is damp and cool, so Lily grabs an afghan for her feet. She twirls the stem of her wineglass between thumb and forefinger.

So I was told to keep my trap shut.

Effective technique, says Phoebe Dinkins, for a teacher. Maybe take up mime.

Lily snorts. Might as well. Libov says I better not discuss Spadina in class again.

But you teach civics!

Exactly what I said. And I was told to keep my opinions to myself.

Phoebe takes a good glug of wine and her tongue turns groovy: A lesson in suppression!

Be serious, Pheeb. How the fuck are these kids going to learn the value of citizenship if they see me cave so quickly?

Phoebe at the hi-fi abides the rhetorical. Reads the liner notes on *Out to Lunch*. She drops the needle, but it skips the groove. Alice the cat leaps out of nowhere.

Shit, says Lily.

The tabby, one-eyed after some ancient scrap, winks.

◊

Two June 2s, forty-five years apart. Your entire lifetime, almost. And in that long span of days, your desire was never to reproduce, but to recreate. To take from the mind's associative clutter hints of rhythmic unity, attach historical tidbit to bookish notions. And now? Now all you hear is the midwife's Doppler measure strong heartbeat, the moment when child and father must both emerge, kicking and screaming.

Es is forty weeks. All signs are good: blood pressure, uterus measurement, heart rate perhaps a little fast. Yours, too. Blood floods your amygdala, increased flow that makes you mindful of every prior moment. The uneasy valence of biography.

◊

In the Blue Cellar Room, where only the stout-armed can serve enormous platters of fried schnitzel, pork chops, and chicken livers. Everywhere glistening carnivorous lips and plates of gristle and bone. Lily and Sachs stick to goulash, split a bottle of Bull's Blood. He finishes his first glass and says, The earliest booksellers were copyists. Did you know that? I'm talking the sixth century or so. They wrote all their books by hand.

Lily takes a sip. Holy Gutenberg! she says.

Sachs gives himself a refill. So here's this poor schmuck, he says, and he's got to copy out *The Consolation of Philosophy* for the sixteenth fucking time. He's working by candlelight, his hand's cramping like crazy, and he says, Screw you, Boethius! And sticks some of his *own* sentences in there.

And they're recorded for posterity, says Lily. Have you read Mumford?

Sachs tops her up. Uh-huh, he says.

He says the city lives by remembering, that its true value comes from how well it can pass on its culture to the next society.

Right.

Lily leans back in her chair, such naked laughter. You *haven't* read Mumford, have you? C'mon. Tell me the truth.

Sachs smiles. Make me, he says.

Veins of frost on the windowpane, but his pad heats up fast. She's on top, commands a slow, steady rhythm. Her sibilant obscenities. He tries to hold back his words as he holds back his climax. No longer. They come not quite together, but not very far apart either.

◊

When you were a boy, people always remarked how much you looked like him. Nothing specific, they said, just something about you. The older you got, the greater the resemblance. Both of you skinny with squinty grey eyes. The same thin chicken legs, the same laugh lines around the mouth. The same laugh, like a last gasp from a collapsed lung.

And like him, your livelihood squirms around a book, a book, another book. A writer and a seller, a pair of marginal characters on opposite ends of a business that now choicelessly meet in the middle.

◊

Histamine snore gives him a start. Heavy-lidded, his eyes loll. Lily is tangled in the sheets. Her boozy breath. Coherence comes with one long slow inhale. He holds a lungful. The bedroom is windowless, but midmorning sounds – delivery-truck honk and hiss, bark of mongers – are well underway. *When was the last time he got laid?* More snores from Lily. A minor rustle exposes breast and hip. There are fingertip bruises on her thigh. Sachs spans his hand. Hovers it above. A perfect match.

◊

You know, of course, how this story ends: Lily breaks it off, the expressway is killed, Sachs vanishes. Such violence in those initial actions – to break, to kill. Outcomes of indispute that make it easy for you to imagine how your uncle might choose to hesitate. He lived in a city on the verge. Changes were about to come to his shop, his street. He sat on the fence so long that splinters were inevitable.

◊

Second-period civics, Harbord Collegiate. Lily explains suffrage with textbook efficiency. She sticks to the curriculum, reminds the class that the legal voting age is now eighteen.

You'll be eligible next year, she says.

A hand shoots up. Marla Goldman: pimply, whiny, distraught over glandular delicacies she'll never overcome. So what? she says. It's all just a bunch of baloney.

Lily sits on the edge of her desk. A lot of people feel the same way, she says. Voter turnout is historically low.

See?

Lily folds her arms. Restraint covers her like a rash.

After class, she clomps through Kensington Market. Pushes back against the steady press of people. The market asynchronous and fishy this morning. She makes her way across Baldwin, stays under awnings. The softly falling snow becomes a blizzard of feathers, a memory from when she was six years old: she had a tight grip on her grandmother's hand when she heard the *schoctim* dress down one poor woman who had improperly plucked a chicken. Such squawking. Not just the terrified fowl, but her own terror, which lodged in her throat like a dreamtime scream.

Shvants, her grandmother had said. Why not pay them more than two cents a bird?

Ida Klein had no truck with repression. She found her footing way back in 1912, one of hundreds of Eaton Company garment workers who walked off the job. And then she continued to walk – out on her wayward husband. She raised her son with a rabble-rouser's aplomb and, when Sid proved to be as feckless in love as his father, raised Lily as well. The two women share both pallor and mien, a sharp-tongued resiliency that ended with Ida's aphasia. Five years ago, she suffered a stroke that left her without speech. Lily visits her twice a week.

In the atrium of the nursing home, the hoary and the hoarse. A young doctor gets cornered by a jut-jawed babushka, her cane wobbles as her voice rises. Someone spills juice on the floor. A quartet of *alta kockers* trade cackles. Lily turns her head toward a wheelchair squeal and sees her grandmother swivel window-ward. Lily pulls up a hard plastic chair and pulls an orange out of her pocket. Peels it. Feeds an eighth. Ida looks at Lily with big silent eyes. Juice runs down her chin.

Chew, Gram, you have to chew.

◊

Your earliest memory is assembled out of moments from that day – the day your mother filed a missing-persons report. Your parents sat at the kitchen table. They never did this except at mealtime. Their sentences, incomplete, carried strange weight.

Maybe he, said your father. His sandbag face shifted with unspoken gravity.

Oh, Larry.

Vacation, you know? With her.

Without telling me? He'd never.

For chrissakes, Min.

You stood in the doorway. Bugs Bunny hijinks on the tube behind you. Commercial time came and you wanted a glass of milk. Your mother took notice: *Did you get peanut butter on the couch again?* Her words were ragged, the facecloth rougher than usual in her hands. Your father picked up the phone, paused.

Larry. Call.

The dial tone was the loudest thing in the room.

More cartoons. The opening credits of *Super Friends* had just begun when the doorbell rang. The police officer was very tall. He wore his shoes in the house. He had one big eyebrow.

The witnesses were all reliable. A man who fit his description was spotted, late in the night, on the Queen East streetcar. He was also seen at Union Station, under the rotunda of the Great Hall, luggageless. One driver swore he appeared on the shoulder of Lakeshore Boulevard, illuminated by the onrush of headlights. His thumb was out.

Your mother was certain about one thing: *He would never hitchhike.* She would explain this to neighbours, relatives, reporters. As though the danger of a stranger's car caused her more grief than the fact that her brother had vanished without a word. At least that was the kind of trouble that could be pinned down. But as the days passed, all explanations hardened into mere recital. The house grew grave. Sobs and nods. Even your father, rarely tight-lipped, muttered but brief asides. *Right in the kishkas*, he'd say, or *Backroom shenanigans.*

He was shushed often.

Something in the impenetrable adultness of those two little words: *the backroom.* You were too young to attach any meaning beyond simple aural significance, but with age came the sound of hushed and lurid antics, the unmistakable murmur of bad behaviour. Montaigne writes of the need for an *arrière boutique*, a metaphorical room behind the shop where the truest self can grab a seat. He also wrote that there is *more wildness in thinking than in lust.*

◊

The next day, nearly sundown. The Jewish shops close early, observant merchants head home. Sachs, too, locks up and rushes to his apartment upstairs. Lily is already there. Her laughter is soft but certain, like the sound of an unbuttoned blouse as it hits the floor. Up and down the street, neighbours prepare for the Sabbath, while these two, apostates both, eschew foreplay. She is wet, prehensile, and makes a mitzvah of sucking his cock.

◊

There is a photo from your mother's wedding that she has never liked: Min in white gown, her eyes flash-red. She gestures with a glass, but her brother appears to be distracted by something just outside the frame. In the time it took for the shutter to open and close, he became a blur.

You were ten years old and had no one to play with. In the backyard, you went into the windup. Threw the tennis ball against the wall and caught it off the bounce. Strike two! This was a familiar game, one played in the head with oneiric facility. You were almost through the imagined batting order before your mother held the screen door ajar. Hinge grate and a jumble in her throat: I've told you a million times! Don't throw the ball against the wall.

You blinked.

Now come inside and wash up.

You pounded the pocket of your mitt, dallied here and there, and hit the kitchen. Your father chomped a radish.

What's up, kiddo?

I dunno.

The table set not quite the same as always. Beyond the salad bowl, in between the napkin holder and breadbasket, sat a *yahrzeit* candle. An all-day flame lit in memory of a man who had finally, seven years after he vanished, been declared dead. You watched it shimmy on the wick.

Pass the butter, said your father.

Twelve years later, another commemorative, another all-day candle. Your mother opened a box of Kleenex. Behind blown honker, she attempted to parse out her brother.

His problems began with that woman, said Min. I believe that. I really do.

She stuffed a wad of tissue into the cuff of her blouse and continued: I mean, I know he'd always had his moods. I'd go weeks without getting him on the phone. And when I did, it was as if nothing happened. He'd never mention it. Not a word.

A toilet flushed. Your father's latest tax rant became louder in the hall. You were twenty-two. You had gotten high through an apple on the way uptown. Your mother was ready to set the table. Knives, forks, spoons, her words rattled within the cutlery drawer: *She was a bit of a boozer, you know.*

◊

The next day, Sachs breaks a sweat. Drags a dozen cartons from the backroom before a bitchy sacrum gives him pause. He kneels. Lifts a lid and catches a good whiff of old wood pulp, a thousand prior mornings in his nostrils.

The door opens and in with a gust comes his friend Joe Sharpe. Name matches his tongue, a killer kibbitzer.

On your knees? he says. Good. Pray for guidance.

I'm sure you can offer me some.

Joe grins and runs a forefinger across the dusty top of the register. He's a middleman for Durwood-Grubb, an outfit that has swallowed city blocks whole and spit out rubble. Leases have been ended, evictions ordered. Sachs, a renter of both commercial and residential space, has so far clung with success to the terms of his original tenancy. But, as the expressway decision looms, Joe is sent by his bosses to talk turkey with his stubborn chum.

You think things won't change, he says. You think it'll be business as usual. We're talking five thousand more cars downtown. *Per hour.* That means parking lots, baby. That means millions of dollars in real estate up for grabs.

That means you show up every month with a new spiel.

Joe rubs his chin, an hispidulous deliberation. These guys, he says, they only know dollars and sense. Common sense. They don't know how to deal with a *yutz* like you.

And you do.

I'm just trying to look out for you, pal.

Sachs straightens up with a soft groan. I know, he says. But if you really want to help, go lug those last boxes out here. My back is killing me.

Businessman's lunch at the Victory Burlesque. Joe Sharpe glances stagewise. Chérie LaRue, held over another week, slips off one sheer glove and flings it into the crowd. Sparse noonday chortle.

Grubb, née Gruber, orders the usual and says, Did he sign?

Not yet.

We're sitting on sixty million worth of real estate, Joe.

I know.

My guy's camped out at the Land Registry Office.

I know, says Joe. I'm working on him. I just need more time.

The food arrives. Grubb's got a mouthful of eggroll, Chérie is down to her pasties, tassel-tipped. The Victory was once a theatre where Yiddish actors risked jailtime for their agitprop performances.

What's the holdup? Money? Because you can go up to six, seven if you need.

Nah. It's not the money. It's just how he is. The shop is all he knows.

Well, use your judgment, says Grubb. You've always done a nice job for us.

Joe nods. He dips a chicken ball.

◊

Friday night, uptown. The Aklers have a Buick in the drive and a mezuzah by the door. The table is set for four. They say the *Motzi*, then the *kiddish*. Min serves the soup, ladle on the precipice of a sudden aporia.

Just tell me one thing, says Larry.

Shoot.

Why don't you want to move?

I never said never, says Sachs. I just said maybe later.

Maybes mean bupkes.

C'mon, Larry.

What come on? We've all moved away from there. You're bringing up the rear.

Aitch Akler, three years old and a mouthful of challah, sniggles. His uncle slurps the soup, a passive indolence honed after years of Sabbath dinners at his sister's house. Larry's in automotive, Min protects the furniture with plastic. They're original up-the-hillniks, part of the first wave of affluent couples who moved out of the cramped homes of their Spadina Avenue forebears and into the new, big-lawned bungalows of North York.

Listen, says Larry. There's no percentage in sticking it out. Once the expressway goes through, you'll lose all your leverage.

If it goes through.

Puh-leese. They've spent what? Thirty million already? Of course they're going to finish it.

So what do you suggest?

Shut it down and come work for me.

Auto parts, says Sachs. I don't even like to drive.

Min in the kitchen fixes a platter of gefilte fish. In the arrangement of jellied patties a deep appeal, her homemaker's id fully satisfied with the preparation of an appetizer. Back at the table, though, it's a different kettle of fish. How many times has her husband tried to nudge her unnudgeable brother? Not that he shouldn't *try*, of course. The bookshop has long been in the red and no one has a better head for business than Larry. Min looks around: where did she leave the tongs?

We own half of that store, don't forget.

She owns half, says Sachs.

You know what I mean: we're entitled to have our say.

Min's back in, lugging the same old words. Nothing in her diction has ever been up to this task. Her advice unheeded, her concern misinterpreted. Theirs is a sibling relationship of eager queries and offhand responses. He might mention a dinner date six months past or a first edition found and sold, but his elaborations were all mumbles and shrugs.

We just want you to think of the future, she says.

Someone's got to, says Larry.

Maybe you should lay off the Manischewitz, says Sachs.

This gets Aitch's attention. He hears humour in the remark, but also ellision, the mystery of missing meaning. These are the absences he will forever try to fill. He furrows his brow and stuffs a tremendous piece of bread into his mouth.

Honey, says Min. Don't be such a chazzer.

The boy's reply is doughy: whaddachazzer?

Larry leans forward. His tie tastes his soup. At least let me make some calls, he says.

Larry knows a lot of people, says Min.

Sachs sees his cloth napkin has slipped from his lap to the floor. He reaches under the table.

Ma! Whadda! Chazzerrrrr!

Friday night, downtown. Expressway fighters from all over town gather at Grossman's Tavern. They dig the turned-on music and twenty-five-cent suds, but burble dissent when a civil rights lawyer named Blatnyck clears his throat. In braying tone, he updates them on the board hearings and outlines expert deputation on driving times, air pollutants, traffic flow. He's a litigious bore and even adamant ears soon sag. A poli-sci student named Irving raises his hand.

Does anyone really believe the OMB will side with us over Metro?

Alderman Ying Hope opens his mouth, but Blatnyck bleats about due process. All opposition groups, he says, have agreed to follow proper legal recourse.

Phoebe Dinkins nods her head. She works reception for the lawyer; she types maybe twelve words a minute, but she only needed to give one drunken handjob to get gainful employment. Across from her, unkempt artist Vern Dyson makes eyes at Lily. Lily rolls her eyes. Irving and boyfriend Claude mutter about the bourgeoisie.

Architect Paul Bosos stands up and says, Listen, people. This is beyond class politics. How many diverse groups have come together on this? It's pure democracy.

If it's so democratic, why not vote on it?

Votes, says the old barber Gus Bosetti. If votes changed anything, they'd make it illegal. Know who says that?

Emma Goldman, says Lily.

Sì, says Gus. She tell me that many times.

You knew her?

Hey! says Vern Dyson. Did I tell you I'm living in her old apartment?

Lily gives him a look.

No guff, he says. You should come check it out.

Stronzo! says Gus. I've been there.

Not you!

◊

Group B streptococcus screening, nonstress test, contraction stress test: Es aced them all. And then, as a transducer roamed her abdomen, an image, almost ectoplasmic, of your child emerged. Sound waves shaped a head and face and hands. It was easy to count all ten fingers, all ten toes.

Hm, said the technician.

You cocked an eyebrow.

The baby was full of gas, intestinal density that somehow left an acoustic shadow across the genitals. There was no way to determine gender.

The technican clicked off the machine and said in a heavy Slavic tone: You will have to wait for the sex.

So: maybe a girl, maybe a boy. This missing piece of infor-mation has helped forestall the future. In all the time that remains, you never once wonder who this new person will be. Rather, you pace, every morning you pace. Bedroom, hall-way, kitchen, where you eat your yogourt and granola. Es put the ultrasound picture on the fridge. You stare and stare: small curled fingers, prominent nose, unfused skull. June 2. You hold your spoon mid-bite, the you of now. *Gone*, wrote William James, *in the instant of becoming.*

◊

Alice the cat hops onto the kitchen table. Sashays under Lily's nose, then sniffs a stack of mid-terms. Picks up the scent of garbled expression, students hip to the flummery of others and yet oblivious to their own. Lily has lost plenty of red ink to lax grammar. Circles awkward structure. She strokes the cat's tail.

What do *you* think of voter apathy, missy?

Phoebe comes in and opens the fridge door. Stares into the dull electric hum.

How's it going?

Ugh, says Lily. Every sentence ends with a preposition. Tough to deal with.

Har-har.

Ready to go?

Almost.

Phoebe pulls out fuzzy cheddar, a jar of something gone green. She opens a carton of milk and sniffs. Her exophthalmic surprise. Guess we'll grab a bite on the way, she says.

There's a deep bone chill outside Stull Electronics as they buzz the apartment upstairs. Brief chatter by the TV tubes.

Pheeb, why are we here?

He insisted.

Inside, they shrug off jackets. Noses running, headlights flashing, neither woman can settle. Palette and oils on the fuliginous sofa, the armchair covered in crumbs. Lily's stomach grumbles, her voice rises.

Lay it on me, she says.

Vern Dyson encompasses the dump with a sweeping gesture. She lived here after the States kicked her out, he says. I thought: you're such a fan of hers, you'd want to see it.

Lily fingers a crack on the wall and strolls around. The room unhaunted. No essence of the old anarchist seeps from vent or fixture, no hint of long-dead Emma Goldman goes *pssst* in her ear.

Vern Dyson hands them each a beer and says, I love her line about the creative person's resistance to all forms of conversion.

Coercion.

Sheesh, he says. You've sure done your homework.

Lily pops an ov. I'm no schoolgirl, she says.

◊

Consider this: only one day after he disappeared – June 3 – the government made it official. The Spadina Expressway was dead. Perhaps this would have made a difference. Perhaps the certainty imposed by this decision could have slowed just enough the speed of his city and left him without the need for reinvention. Or not. Maybe he was no longer able to stall. Maybe he had reached the limits of his geography.

When he disappeared, he was the same age as you are now.

◊

She stands at the big corner. Signs float above the broad avenue, flashy enticements for Neilson Chocolate and the Silver Dollar Room are in strong relief to the overcast sky. Below, sedans and cabs clog the intersection; they bleat and screech, bleat and screech, but who cares where they go because the real action is curbside. Endless migrations up and down Spadina. The steady beat of untold footfalls, sidewalk pulse that steers a sample-case schlepper through the crosswalk at College, that keeps a cadre of Guyanese *shmatte* workers gossiping outside the Crescent Grill. This vast block shaking with negotiation, gesticulation, ejaculation.

What kind of city do you want? says Lily. She stands under the neon palm tree of the El Mocambo Tavern, handing out leaflets. Easy rhythm in the way she peddles her papers. Lays one on a northbound minister, hip and guitar-slung, then foists another on a young hard hat heading the opposite way. Metro wants bigger roads. Bigger buildings. Bigger contracts. And what do we want?

Passersby are all ears.

We want to be heard!

A mildewed pair crosses her path. Matron in furs, droopy-eyed gent who pulls out a pince-nez to glance at the tract, sniff, then toss it away like a soiled hanky. Lily stands there, suddenly speechless. Flakes of snow begin to fall. She sticks out her tongue.

Wet snow. Tremendous globs of the stuff for two days straight. Over and over Spadina shovels out, the sidewalk fetishistically clean just in case some schmuck slips on his bean and decides to sue. So, all down the avenue truculent jobbers heft and heave, as do the truant kids who breathlessly make a buck the hard way. Boy in a blue parka digs out Cecil Street Books.

Sachs looks out the window and sees Lily approach. Curvaceous breath, the swivel of hips. She eyes him eyeing her and comes in with the last of her pamphlets.

Still waiting for you to make that offer, she says.

Sachs sniffs the fresh ditto. Sweet aniline purple!

The blue-parkaed boy comes in and stamps off his boots. All done, Mr. S.

Sachs hits a button on the register and the cash drawer pops open. Okay, Luis. Go get yourself a pop.

The sign on the shop door says: *Back in 5 Minutes.*

It's a hasty love.

After, he walks her through an aisle in History. Stands in the spot where his father had died while shelving an unabridged Pepys.

Boom, says Sachs. His heart.

So you helped run the place?

He nods. Unlocks the door.

And, says Lily, you've never done anything else.

Sachs shrugs. It was always going to be temporary, he says, until it wasn't.

◊

Last week, you rode the subway uptown. Your gaze, clear and reflective, grew diffuse when the train emerged from the tunnel. The route north of Eglinton runs along a shallow open cut, meridian for the truncated expressway. Traffic on either side was fender-to-fender. You got off at Lawrence West and put on sunglasses for the short walk to her condo.

Television voices came loud and clear from the other side of the door. You didn't bother to ring the bell because her hearing is bad no matter what the volume. You let yourself in and stood in the hallway until your mother became aware of your presence.

Is everything okay? she said.

Everything's fine, Ma. Es is fine. She's at home.

You should be with her. What if she needs you?

Then she'll call.

Cellphones, she said, as if this settled the matter. She was uneasy about the home birth, the absence of an OB. Unnerved by the jinxed due date and your apparent calm. You were raised to expect the worst and she could only shake her head at your obtuse denial of heredity.

I knew she'd be late, said your mother.

You said early.

I did not.

Yup. When the baby dropped into position, you told us to get ready for an early birth.

I don't remember.

I do.

She patted the couch. Why are we even arguing about this? Come sit.

You sat.

So, tell me, she said. Have you assembled the crib yet?

You have this sense of yourself as someone with no future, that the upcoming days will assert themselves in ways you will not be able to integrate. This is a failure of imagination. You're well-versed in the present tense, a tension between the action in your head and the sentences you emit into the world. The past is something you're eager to disassemble and reassemble. But you have no language for what is to come. Your standard line is you're *prepared to be unprepared.*

You don't, of course, believe a word of it.

Es ached. She reminded you of the trigger points that promote labour: inside of the leg, three finger widths above the ankle. A tender spot on the trapezius. She sipped lemon verbena, called by the midwife a cervical opening tea. She also suggested spicy food and sex. Five nights in a row, tofu vindaloo cooled on the table.

◊

Joe Sharpe heads up the steps of a D'Arcy Street house. His index finger hits the buzzer, but the plate is unscrewed and the entire contraption pops off its wires. So he knocks. Knocks louder. The second-floor flat leased to the Malinga brothers. They're hard workers; two lug pelt for Gilman's Furs, another pulls double shift for a cab company. The youngest one opens the door. He's out of work, has a fat lip.

What happened to you?

The kid waves his hand in a manner that could mean anything.

Listen, says Joe. You guys got to clear out of here. Sorry. The city inspector's on my case. I need to rewire the whole place.

This is a lie, of course; Joe's got another family lined up at fifty bucks more per month. But the kid buys it. His ruined mouth quivers.

Mr. Sharpe. We have nowhere else to go.

Joe's rumination is well-rehearsed. No sweat, pal. I've got a vacancy coming up on Baldwin. A day or two, tops. Just have to roust a few deadbeats.

Yeah?

Sure. It's a little cozier than what you got now. But, y'know.

The youngest Malinga nods. Joe slaps him on the shoulder. Good, he says. I'll drop off the keys Thursday. You guys'll be out by Friday, right?

Two more houses on D'Arcy, then three on Baldwin. Joe rents ten a month from Grubb, then leases out the rooms himself. He clears two grand. The only trick is to keep the city from nosing around. Bylaw infractions cost time and money. Sure, he's got both, but not enough to squander willy-nilly. He checks his watch. He's got no stomach for the rest of the street: welfare mom and her moon-faced brood, the heavy smoker who sets his bedsheets on fire. More palatable perhaps is Mrs. Mintz. The old lady's lived on Cecil all her life, but between the noisy neighbours, the cockroaches, and the influx of Chinese, she might be nudged enough to sell. She answers the door with a sneeze. Wears a toque and scarf and her bathrobe.

Verkakte radiator. Mr. Sharpe, would you mind having another look?

Sure thing, says Joe. He smiles. He'd never do this for one of his own tenants, but, hey, block-busting is an art, not a science.

◇

Sachs prefers slim masterpieces, but lies down with the fat ones. *Portable Faulkner*, say, or *The City in History*. They rest on his chest, such a comforting heft. He likes to sleep with his books before reading them.

◇

You once spoke with Lily Klein. This was twenty years after the expressway was cancelled. After your uncle vanished. She was, by then, a writer, an urbanist with popular appeal. She had a column in the newspaper. A book that approached the bestseller list. Twice a week, she lectured at Innis College and stumped for the intimacy of the built environment. Superblocks, she argued, had forever damaged the physiognomy of our city. She cited health statistics, Ada Louise Huxtable. She spoke without notes.

After, she shared a chuckle with three students. They left but she remained. Elbows on the lectern, hint of clavicle beneath her pale blue scarf. She removed her half-glasses and looked your way. She squinted hard. You watched her crow's feet deepen with uncertain recognition.

Are you auditing my class?

Un-uh.

She stepped down from the stage with a steady gaze.

You look familiar.

It's been a long time, you said. I was three years old the last time you saw me.

Oh, shit. You look just like him. Does anyone tell you that?

Everyone.

She glanced toward the door. The accumlation of lines in her face, the looser skin, only added to her profile. She was always the most modern of characters – autonomous, fast in her habits – but also someone adept at the uses of disorder. Not unlike the system she despised; capitalism creates and discards. She had declared entire phases of her life obsolete.

You're not a student then?

No.

So, you're here because?

I'm curious.

About him? Like you said: it's been a long time.

I know, you said. But I guess I thought.

Honestly. I don't know anything more now than I did back then. Probably less.

She put her hand on her hip. She was thirty years your senior, but there was a current between you, nothing carnal, simply a charge that ran to where you stood, silently, in your rubber-soled sneakers.

◊

You haven't slept for a week. Or, rather, each night you fall asleep and wake up. Far too early. 3:18, 3:21. Today, 3:13. Your eyelids were up, strict; they denied you even that fuzzy lull between the slumbering mind and a wakeful one. Moonlight peeked through the blinds: Es on her side, the outline of her craterous belly button. You needed to piss. You once read about a study in consciousness: test subjects were woken at various intervals through the night and asked the time. Most were accurate to within twelve minutes. Although they all thought it was later than it actually was. A husband-and-wife team ran the experiment. Their name was Boring.

You were careful and quiet down the hallway. Left the toilet unflushed and continued, light on the heel, to the living room. Big red armchair and floor-lamp corona. Same as the other sleepless nights, the same head trip. A nameless anxiety approaches from far away and you do nothing to get out of the way. You're stuck, transfixed by the near-impact of mute associations.

◊

Sachs is studying the ads in *Antiquarian Bookman* when the phone rings.

I can get you six large, says Joe. Maybe seven.

Yeah?

Is that a yes?

No.

The single syllable hangs on the line, gobby with recall. Joe lets loose a sigh that stretches back half a life. They once sat beside each other in school, and out of this alphabetical convenience grew a decade of matters pursued with the seriousness of chess prodigies: shagging flies like Goody Rosen, jerking off to Jane Russell.

Problem is, pal, you're such a goddamned contrarian. You know this is a good deal so you've gotta run in the other direction. You're scared you'll actually get what you want.

Geez, Joe. Pop pyschology? That's beneath you.

◊

Three nights later, the door to Vern Dyson's pad is ajar so Lily goes in and finds Phoebe, at the window, in a peignoir.

Stark cerulean light and the thin fabric announce aureole and pudenda.

Ooh-la-la, says Lily.

Give me a break.

Vern clomps out of the kitchen. Whiff of turpentine and testosterone. Lumberjack shirt open to the sternum, splatter on the sleeves. He opens a bottle of cheap red.

Whaddya think?

Lily turns to the unfinished caryatid on the canvas. Elongated neck and abstract countenance. Nipples akimbo.

She looks cold.

Never mind that, says Phoebe, now robed. The rally is this weekend. What should our signs say? They're framing this as uptown versus downtown.

It *is* uptown versus downtown.

Tell that to the people in Forest Hill. Tell it to them in Cedarvale.

Exactly! What happens when they want to build the Crosstown? Or the Christie? They'll be tearing up every neighbourhood in town.

And for what? For five minutes and fifty-three seconds. That's what they'll gain.

We need to show them what they'll lose, says Lily. We need something that hits them where they live.

Vern Dyson hands out the brushes and paint, Phoebe does the placards. Lily's words trampoline off the tongue. Her slogan is acrylic, acerbic, and she completes it with a grand looping serif and a great gulp of wine:

Your House Is Next!

Lily hungover at Harbord Collegiate. Last night's bad wine holds her sinuses hostage. Her teeth hurt. She lists the benefits of the electoral process on the blackboard, cusses silently each screech of chalk.

Faye passes a note to Connie. Danny, head in hand, hides the earpiece of his transistor radio. It's the last class on a Friday and the students are no less restless than their teacher. Lily tries not to eye the clock. Tick-tock goes her interest in the syllabus, tick-tock her textbook submission. She palms an apple off her desk. Burnishes it.

Okay, she says. Listen up.

Muttered asides abate, but there are still too many distractions so she captures full attention with a tried-and-true tactic.

Your parents won't like this – she has all their ears now – and Principal Libov has already told me to cool it. But I teach civics. And I can't in good conscience ignore the biggest civics lesson in our lives just because some people are going to wig out on me. Democracy is not just something that we talk about in the classroom. It happens outside. It's happening right now.

She closes in on the front row of desks and chomps her apple. Maybe you've heard about the big rally tomorrow, she says.

From the four corners they come, braving rude Fahrenheit and the uncertain allure of a grassroots movement. Hundreds of determined footfalls traverse icy fossa, trample traditional class lines: Chinatown grocer and U of T radical, Annex ratepayer and the wife of a Kensington Market fishmonger.

They keep coming and coming, solidarity growing with each step. They stuff the sidewalk, jam the street, and then converge, as planned, in the middle of College and Spadina.

The wide intersection quickly becomes shoulder-to-shoulder. What's the deal? says a cabbie on his coffee break. But the retort is cut short by a blast of feedback and the bodies that hoick and scooch beside him. He stands on tiptoes and sees, beyond all the toques and placards, a man with a megaphone. This is Powell, chair of the STOP! movement. He marshals the crowd through chants and static.

And we will not *ka-zzzt* because our future is *daa-zat* to save our city!

Mittened fists rattle like sabres. Lungfuls of air explode into frosty words.

SAVE OUR CITY! SAVE OUR CITY!

This short sentence, anthemic, surges forward even as the crowd gets pushed back. Bus 77, with an escort of mounted police, winds around Spadina Crescent and rolls unimpeded down the street. Scattered cheers for public transit go silent when an Oldsmobile tries to take advantage of the egress. Several protesters jump forward. The Olds jolts to a stop. The driver hammers his horn. Lily raps the hood. SAVE OUR CITY! SAVE OUR CITY! Someone kicks a hubcap and the police horse neighs and the contours of people shift over and over, a buzzing tremendum captured by both the television cameras and the deep-set eyes of Hal Sachs. He rests an elbow on the register.

Look at this *mishegas*, says Mrs. Mintz. They should mind their own business.

She takes tiny sensible steps toward the cash. Her face baggy like old nylons. She pecks at her crocheted change purse and counts out coins. Thirty-five, sixty, seventy.

Sachs is patient as landscape. Glances up idly just as Lily enters the shop. It's a seismic moment. In the crazy avalanche of seconds, Mrs. Mintz, triumphant, hits her total while the roar of approval over the blocked car reaches apo - theosis. Lily plants a big one on Sachs, their backs to the fray and the snowflakes that start to fall, like confetti.

Can't beat the scene at Grossman's. Not just because the first round is on the house, but because the congratulatory vibe continues long after the rally has ended. *Democra-shee*, goes the toast.

Lily, half in the bag, weaves around the revellers with a pitcher of beer. She refills Gus Bosetti's glass, then ones for Phoebe and Sachs.

So, she says, they hassled you?

Sì, says Gus. Like criminals they treat us. Not even three words I can say to my *paisan* before bang-o, the *polizia* is tapping me on the shoulder. English, they say, it is the law you speak English.

What'd you say?

To them I say *vaffanculo*, pigs! Well, they get rough. That is how I get this — he points to a pale scar above his lip — and this — to a paler twin on his wispy pate.

Shit, Gus. That smarts.

Sì. Smarts like a fox. Because that night I see she is moved by my wounds. She is older than me, a woman of the world.

She see – how you say – the big picture. She say to me, Agostino, there is no revolution. Only one moment of a long, hard evolution.

She who? says Sachs.

Emma Goldman, says Phoebe.

Lily smiles a tipsy smile. They called her the most dangerous woman in the world.

Sì. Because she speak with fire. To get out the word, everything she does is with fire. *Passionate.*

Gus! Are you blushing?

Gus looks at the floor. Looks up. With a hand that has shaved thousands unnicked, he shakily taps a spot on his neck.

She kiss me here. Hard.

Hard?

Sì.

Are you trying to tell us that Emma Goldman gave you a hickey?

Gus drains the rest of his beer in one gulp. I say too much already.

Come on, says Lily. How far'd you get? First base? Second base?

◊

Min does the books. On the last Sunday of every month, she sits in her brother's kitchen and taps out small agonies on the adding machine. She checks her numbers, sighs, rechecks them.

Sachs at the counter chops an egg. Sales are always down in the winter, he says. You know that.

They were down in the fall, too.

Taxi receipts, plumbers'. One from a pizza parlour. So many expenses for such a small operation. There is a hand-written bill for general labour she needs to read twice.

This is made out to you and not the business.

Uh-huh.

Plus, your name is spelled wrong. You need to be accurate with all this. How am I supposed to make any sense of it all?

Sachs struggles with a jar of mayonnaise. He runs the lid under hot water, whacks it with a wooden spoon. Comes to the table with a plate of sandwiches. His sister sorts more paper and sharpens her pencil: double-entry accounting can be a singular pain.

This is what I mean, she says. Look at this.

He leans over her shoulder. Min sees him squint at the ledger.

When's the last time you had your eyes checked? she asks.

◊

Minutes to go before first period. Commotion in the halls, kissing. A girl in owl rims gives her boyfriend a pat on the ass. A trig book bonks the floor and two twelfth-graders guffaw. Somewhere, the reverb of a basketball.

Hey! Miz K!

Lily turns to see Pammy DaSilva. Long, long hair and a leather trench with a *Stop Spadina!* button in the lapel. She taps it twice and and gives the thumbs up.

Lily watches her go.

The bell rings. Lockers creak and slam and then there's Principal Libov, looking steamed.

She's suspended without pay. Grabs her coat from the staff room, where drama and gym teacher offer only downturned eyes. The hallway is so, so long. The janitor gives his usual grunt. She goes outside and does not look back. Not at the arched entranceway nor at the students who grab a quick smoke. Lily on the sidewalk has a spasm in the diaphragm, tear ducts on the verge.

She walks. Angry breath behind her, visible and twisted. Her cheeks flush with rage and cold. She stomps down Manning to College. *Mannink*, Ida would say with Yiddish inflection, *Cullig*. Back when she could speak. Lily shivers: her grandmother forced into a permanent silence. Not the same fate for the granddaughter, no way. She continues east, the businesses on this stretch all Italian — a record shop with Tito Schipa albums on sale, the Riviera Bakery. Red light at Bathurst. A fogged-up Plymouth makes a wide left. She cuts down Lippincott. Families from the Azores live here, recent arrivals who moved into staid Victorians and repainted them aquamarine, coral. The Mediterranean hues a visual respite from deep winter. Water crystalizes in Lily's lashes. She avoids the hustle of Kensington Market, the hawkers and hagglers, and instead follows a more solitary route, the soft eastward curve along Dundas.

Below Dundas, below Queen, below Wellington. She ditches imperial nomenclature, Bolshevik countenance, stray thoughts. The Balfour building, the Darling: nothing but concrete figments. She slows, briefly, in front of Clarence Square – site of many May Day rallies – before continuing over the railyards toward the water. Lily stands at the municipal edge. Fists in her pockets. The mercury drops, her heart sinks. What now?

What now? says Sachs.

Lily blows on her hands. Her diaphragm continues to jump, every sentence sliced by a hiccup.

Beats – me.

Do you think it's personal?

With Libov? Un-uh. He's just – y'know – a func – tionary.

Maybe you can appeal then. To the school board or the trustee or whoever makes the decision.

No fucking – way! I took a stand and – I'll take – the conse – sequen – ces.

Don't go all Simone Weil on me.

She smiles. I won't starve.

Sachs grabs a bottle off the kitchen counter, pours two stiff ones, and returns to the table. Formica-topped, short-legged, it wobbles enough to leave tiny splashes of Old Grand-Dad here and there.

Take a swig, he says. But don't swallow. Hold it in your mouth till I count to ten.

They clink.

One Mississauga, two Mississauga, three Mississauga.

Lily's cheekbones dot pink. Her eyes widen.

Four Mississauga, five Mississauga.

Her brow furrows, a tickle in the nose.

Six Mississauga, seven Mississ –

Gah! says Lily. She holds out her glass.

Hit me – again.

They down half the bottle. Badinage off the tongues turns thick. They take off their clothes, hop in the shower, and it is there, drunken, sudsy, impulsive, that he asks her to move in with him.

◊

One month! They date for one month and she moves in? What kind of woman does that?

You put a pencil dot on the living room wall of your mother's new condo. You were almost forty, attuned for the moment to the word *date* that lolled in your ear. The verb had become quaint, its delicacy resistant to the next burst of sororal ferocity.

Who did she think she was? your mother said.

You responded with hammer whams. One, two.

You picked up a framed photo of your father. Thick black glasses, receding hairline. He was very tanned. On his face some mid-career mix of satisfaction and resignation. He'd been buried not five months before the old house was sold and you came uptown to help your mother move in. She set her jaw tight. Shelving paper needed to be laid, lampshades dusted, pictures hung.

And did she ever go back to teach school? Nosiree. Too proud. But not too proud to sponge off him the whole time.

She assessed your job. She furrowed her brow. Too high, she said.

◊

The first thing Lily does is find space for the litter box. She shoves the shower curtain aside and fills the pan. Calls. Alice sniffs in and out of corners, detects nothing feline in the many foreign scents of this new apartment. Slowly, sedulously, she covers the vast terrain of the living room.

Kitten? says Lily. Where are you?

Nothing to do but wait. She has little else to do, few things to claim. Her typewriter sits in its case beside a bureau, duffle bag still packed on the bed. Lily on her haunches. She calls again and the cat trots in. Sniffs and purrs. Alice shits in her box and then paws her business. Lily opens the window a crack and cold winter air enters the room.

The second thing she does is stand in the middle of the sitting room. Sun-up. Daylight alternates pink and grey against the window, an unfastened wall sconce on the sill.

Baseboard dust. Small piles of books run the floor, titles he brings upstairs to read and takes back down to sell: Kenko and a Cohen and someone named Ethel Wilson. There's a cover-torn copy of *The Hustler* and, slipped between a pair of fat pocketbooks, one slender hardcover. She reaches for it. *Of Being Numerous*, only sixty-four pages – Perfect! she whispers out loud. She strides into the kitchen, where she kneels and slides the book under the uneven table leg. She gives a small shake, but nothing, nada, not a wobble.

Joe Sharpe fishes for change. He dials. Behind the pay phone, three generations of jobbers close up shop. A dewlapped convoy, they trudge carton after carton out of their old store-front and into a rented van. The foot traffic idles. Pedestrians and familiars congregate with the merchant family. A beat cop jaws with the middle son. Joe looks over his shoulder and says into the receiver, Yup. Uh-huh. Almost.

Street-corner divestment. Durwood-Grubb purchased this five-store complex in late fall and four commerical tenants packed it in before snowfall. Big City Jobbers is the last to go.

The crowd disperses. The last box is loaded. Joe rubs his temple and walks over to the door and tapes a *No Trespassing* sign inside it.

Sachs takes the morning to doll up his display window. Lustig covers only, the New Directions titles that always sell well. He grabs off the shelf a copy of *Confessions of Zeno*, with its reticulated portrait of a face aflame. Picks a Boyle.

Black-blue-and-grey lithograph of a poison bottle and uncertain spiral printed on off-white wove paper. He whistles while he works. *Three Lives, Paterson, A Season in Hell*. He needs as much time to ogle the books as he does to arrange them.

Third, she unzips her duffle. Spreads her duds on the mattress. Tights with a run, an ill-folded blouse. Lily presses on a crease and the box spring squeaks, déjà vu moment for a woman whose history includes numerous strange beds. She straightens up, effort in each vertebra, and lets loose a long sigh.

Dull headache up and down the stairs. Eighteen steps each flight, two flights per building, six buildings on this block and four more across the street. Joe has never bothered to add them up; he saves his rudimentary arithmetic for the calculations of rent. Most of these tenants owe money yet they are always the ones who put *him* on the spot. Broken windows, leaky pipes, electrical shorts. They all have their problems, so he nods, listens, does nothing because it's rent day and his job is not to give but take. He takes money from the indignant artist, the indigent trucker, the inebriated tanner. He does not give a receipt, doesn't give out his phone number, gives not a single assurance of repair – there is no incentive to fix anything in a building soon to be demolished. He is simply the middleman. His bosses count bills in one hand and blasting caps in the other.

Ka-ching!
Ka-boom!

Happy hour in the Cabana Room, second floor of the Spadina Hotel. The bartender has a Zapata moustache, the waitress bunions. She sits on a stool and massages her foot when Joe Sharpe shows up.

Wish you'd let me treat you to some Dr. Scholl's, Gretch.

The waitress shows her dimples. Pineapple earrings dangle. Big spender, she says. Shot and a beer?

Please.

Joe unrolls the newspaper from the pocket of his overcoat and lingers but a moment over city hall coverage before he opens the sports. He knocks back his whisky and releases a soft hiss.

Bum a smoke?

She proffers him one. He lights up, the flickering orange of promises made and broken. He's quit three times before. He watches Gretchen stand and straighten out her silk dress. Foliage printed on the bodice. She's short and bosomy, a figure he'd figured out long ago.

What time do you get off? he says.

Lastly, that night in bed. Sachs has his back to her, asleep, and Lily becomes a student of nape and scapula and spine.

◊

This morning, not quite eight. Kitchen light a worry on the retinas. Everything in sight – blister pack of Celexa, fruit bowl — pouched your eyes. You leaned against the counter and peeled a banana. Es rolled out of bed and, with resonant thal-umphs, made her way. She eased herself into a chair.

No sleep? she said.

Some.

You started to scalp a half-dozen strawberries. Pulled out yogourt from the fridge. Do you want oatmeal with this? Or avocado toast?

Both. Can you get me a glass of water, too? I'm really thirsty.

You're not getting dehydrated, are you?

Es gave her belly a consolatory pat. Your papa's a worrier, she said.

She'll find that out soon enough.

She?

You shrugged. The kettle whistled. Although her designs were on breakfast, Es opted, with impressive effort, to raise herself out of the chair and come kiss your unshaven cheek. Why don't you get out of the apartment for a while? she said. Go for a bike ride. Go for a coffee.

◊

Sachs turns on the tube. Reception comes and goes. He unrolls the foil from his TV dinner and faces an explosion of steam. He pushes his peas around. *Go Spadina! Go!* The voice-over mentions OMB *appeal* and *Cabinet approval,* terms that limp out despite the announcer's deep melisma. Sachs fiddles with the rabbit ears until the picture becomes clear: unemployed construction workers are protesting outside city hall. *Go Spadina! Go!* Hal shifts, a lump of Salisbury steak in his throat.

Lily and Phoebe go door-to-door. Humewood has a strong ratepayers' association, homeowners scared of appropriation. But it's dinnertime, so they get several polite *No*s. A slam or two. They stand under a great bare maple. Hint of sleet in the air.

Maybe we should cut out early.

Lily checks her clipboard. Let's finish this block, she says.

Phoebe tucks her chin into her scarf. All day she'd banged out affadavits – a bathhouse roust, piddly possession charges – with Blatnyck over her shoulder. He's all moony over me, y'know.

I know.

Took him three times to clear his throat before he asked me out.

Lily snorts. What'd you say?

I said: Go home to your wife, Karl.

Geez.

I think I'm going to quit.

Lily nudges her along. They wind up a slippery drive, Phoebe steadies herself against the front of a wood-panelled station wagon. Three small icicles hang off the licence plate.

How're you going to make the rent? I still feel lousy cutting out on you.

Phoebe squeezes Lily at the elbow. Don't worry about it. Irving's parents finally kicked him out. He and Claude are going to take the second bedroom.

Cozy.

Up the wide stone steps to a big brass knocker. They both reach for it at the same time. What about you? says Phoebe. How do you like living in holy bedlock?

Sachs pops the cork. He bloops wine into their glasses. Lily wraps fingers around hers, palm warmth moves up to wrist and forearm.

What'd Phoebe say?

She says you're a fast mover.

Heh. This is a first for me, y'know.

Shacking up?

He nods. Conjugating, he says.

Like the verb? says Lily. I screw, you screw, we screw.

Sachs smacks his knee. Alice the cat slinks around his legs. Claws the sofa, a tactic only ignored.

What's the present preterite? he says.

Um. We screwed.

The infinitive?

Screw!

Very good. Past participle?

Having screwed.

The cat mewls for attention. Hops onto Lily's lap and looks up with indignation, expectation.

Past perfect?

We had screwed.

Future perfect?

We will screw.

Nope. We will *have* screwed.

Are you sure?

Alice leaps from Lily's lap to his.

Trust me, Sachs says.

◊

The adjudicators at the Ontario Municipal Board had heard all the evidence, new and old. They listened to opinions on adjusted costs, lost productivity. For the hundreth time in his career, Roads Commissioner Cass explained that the success of Spadina would pave the way for the next inner-city expressway, from Highway 401 down toward Christie Pits. An ecology professor exaggerated carbon dioxide levels. An eleven-year-old girl lamented the destruction of her favourite playground. Lawyers on both sides promulgated data. They billed extravagantly. The decision would come any day. The whole goddamned city held its breath.

◊

Middle of the month before the bad weather finally relents. Sun and a slow thaw bring hourly topographical changes to

Spadina. Snowbanks become large seeping puddles, danger-ous passages of icy sidewalk vanish into safer, slushier ground. The big melt transudes even brick: blackish trickles wend the lone exterior wall of Cecil Street Books, soaking three shelves of fiction on the other side.

Sachs hunches over a limp dust jacket. He pats it dry with a sponge, then stands the hardcover upright in the shop's big sunlit window. Lily mops up. There's a silent rhythm to their work, a syntax interrupted when Joe drops in. His tongue unwavering as usual, but it wavers when he tries to place this woman's familiar face.

Sachs does the introduction.

Lily toes her bucket across the floor. Seen you around, she says. You're Grubb's bagman.

Joe's smile is thinner than a vein. I manage some properties around here, he says and then turns to Sachs: I thought you ran a solo operation.

Lily flops her mop. He's not my *boss.*

Triangled glances and the moment runs lonely and wayward, like a trickle of sweat.

I stand corrected, says Joe. He rolls up his sleeves. Give you a hand?

Joe stays for dinner. Yesterday's chili, a plate of cornbread whipped up quick. A beeswax candle brightens the room. Something itches his eyes, the dander of domesticity. He turns to Lily. Do you have a cat?

Are you allergic?

It's mild. He clears his throat. So, he says, what kind of city *do* you want?

An inclusive one, Lily says. One that doesn't mess with people's homes, with their livelihoods.

Honey, it already does.

Don't call me *honey*.

Sorry. All I'm saying is you got cars clogging residential streets, you got trucks stuck god-knows-where trying to deliver goods.

So the solution is to tear out the middle of the city?

Joe's nose twitches. Ah-choo!

Sachs forks his beans. Bless you.

Listen, says Joe. Progress has a price.

Easy for you to say: you aren't paying it.

True. But that's because I was smart enough to get out in front of this deal. Unlike some.

Sachs bites and chews. The table cozy as a toothache. Y'know, he says, Joe's folks ran a cigar shop on Dundas.

Lily dabs the corner of her mouth with a napkin. Oh yeah?

Joe nods. Yup. Near Huron. Though the real business was in back: a numbers bank. Nothing major, but enough to parlay into a mortgage payment.

The odds were what, Joe? Six hundred to one?

For the payoff. Odds of winning were more like a thousand to one. The suckers loved to play the leap year. We used to get hundreds of plays on two-two-nine. They never hit, of course.

For dessert, fruit cocktail from the can. Spoons clink the bottoms of bowls. Joe's done first. Did you hear the province is getting in on the action, he says. They want to take it away from the syndicate. Legalize it. Don't know who scares me more, the crooks or the bureaucrats.

Sachs smiles. Not like the old days, he says. Remember the shmoes that used to work for your dad? Joey Applebaum. Solly Cling. The Volgaysi brothers. Wonder where they are now?

Now? says Joe. He makes a face like a fat man climbing stairs. They're either dead or uptown.

Lily takes a call in the bedroom and leaves the men to clean up. Sachs is wrist-deep in suds. Joe dries a bowl.

She's a real firecracker.

Thought you'd like her.

Joe twirls the dishtowel. Different from the others, too. Like what's-her-name. The milquetoast.

Sachs lifts a pot out of the water and examines a starchy glob on the lip. Ever hear from Dot?

Alice pads near. After protracted study she moves on. Ah-choo! says Joe. In the three years since his ex walked out, he's had plenty of luck with women, most of it bad: possessiveness, spite, penicillin. Nah, he says. That ship has sailed. You, though: I got to admit I never thought I'd see you play house.

Sachs shrugs and hands over a plate. I'm a changed man.

Joe taps his fingernail on the china and says, You missed a spot.

February 17. After sixteen days of hearings, the Ontario Municipal Board voted to approve funds for the continued construction of the Spadina Expressway. It was a split decision, two to one; ironically, the dissenter, chair J. A. Kennedy, had helped pass the original plan back in 1963. The ensuing seven years, he said, had taught him much about the impact of expressways: destruction of neighbourhoods, loss of parkland, air pollution that would reach unendurable levels by 1995.

In order to avoid a civic crisis, he changed his mind.

February 17, later. Sachs in a lather. San Severo Barbershop, two chairs, no waiting. Gus Bosetti puts downs his brush and mug. Lily just broke the news about the OMB. She flips open the afternoon edition of the *Telegram*. Says from behind headlines, No Pasquale today?

The barber shakes his head. Opens his straight razor and takes three steps forward. From sink to chair, he leaves a trail of other men's hair.

No more Pasquale. He stays home. The doctor says he has too much blood in his leg.

Too much blood? Lily looks at the other chair, empty. You mean thrombosis?

Sì. A terrible thing for a barber. All day we stand. This is how I do my job. I cannot cut the hair — he does a quick squat — if I sit.

I'm sorry to hear that, Gus.

Sachs stays silent. Keeps his eyes closed and tilts his head according to Gus's touch. Firm strokes on the right side of his face scrape and scrape and scrape.

Seventeen years we are open here.

I know.

We come on the boat together. To this country. We are boys together. The same town. San Severo. You know where this is? The south.

The boot.

The *heel* of the boot. Like a fancy woman's heel. How you say? Long. Pointy.

Stiletto?

Sì, the stiletto. The heel of the boot of Italy. Ionian Sea. Adriatic Sea.

Gus shifts his feet. Wipes soap off the blade.

I miss the water, he says.

Lily and Sachs arm-in-arm down the street. His face frigid and stung from aftershave. They pass the local screw-up, who trails behind him an empty coat rack and the whiff of reefer. Two teens hit them up for a dollar. There's dog piss in the snow.

She packs a ball of slush and ice and fires at the orange-and-black sign stuck to storefront hoarding: *Dur*-Splat!-*wood*-Splat! *Gru*-Splat!-*bb.*

◊

You lean back and yawn. Rub your eyes. The coffee shop is filled with tweets and chirps, laptop piffle. Everyone up to the minute and even you begin to rouse from the rut of *then*. What next? You do the first thing that comes to mind: order another.

◊

They cram into the small flat, a candlelit five. Disaffected with the state of the Stop Spadina campaign, they arm themselves with scissors and glue and engage in tannin-flecked debate about the need to secede.

Injunctions, says Irving. Affadavits. We're wasting our time with these turkeys.

Agreed, says Claude. The two poli-sci students sit side by side; one clips letters out of an old magazine, the other reshuffles headlines from *Good Housekeeping* into shibboleth. Crumpled memoranda all around them. Pages of legalese. J. J. Robinette, counsel for the Stop Spadina Save Our City Coordinating Committee, filed an appeal with the province. The OMB would not have the last word.

They're fighting the system on its own terms. We need to level the playing field.

How? says Lily.

That's what we're here to decide, says Irving. He lights a Belmont and blows smoke through the room.

Phoebe fans her face. There's a blueprint for stopping expressways, she says. Remember the Lower Manhattan? Jacobs versus Moses?

Speaking truth to power, says Lily.

Exactly, says Phoebe.

If that's your take, says Irving, why are you here?

I *live* here, remember.

Vern Dyson burps. He rolls up his sleeves and says, I think what she's trying to say –

I can speak for myself, Vern!

– is that, uh –

Lily's voice rises, a febrile lilt. You want to splinter. Don't you?

I want to be part of a group that *does* something.

You can't just break off suddenly.

Why not? says Claude

We'd need a name, Vern says. Something snappier than ss-soccc.

Gee, says Phoebe. That's a puzzler.

How about the Guerrilla Army of Spadina?

Great. The papers'll call us GAS.

Irving grinds out his butt. Who cares what the papers say?

Listen, says Lily. We've all invested a lot of time in building up the movement.

For all the good it's done.

It's done plenty of good. Public opinion has definitely shifted.

Yeah, but public opinion alone won't cut it. We need to tackle private interest. We need to consider more aggressive tactics.

Lily leans forward. What did you have in mind?

PART TWO

Caffeine jag under a high sky. The second espresso was ill-advised. There's an anxious jump in your step, an out-of-the-Market stride that takes you back to Spadina in no time. You wait to cross, toe-tap. Streetcars south and north. Two women – one with a walker, the other a pale blue parasol – attempt to figure out the fare machines. Your phone is almost out of juice. You text Es again and tell her you are about to head home.

◊

Two copies of *The Bad Trip* on display at the cash. A browser on her knees searches for hidden gems. Sachs stares out the window, eyes maunder around the foot traffic on Spadina

Avenue. Day after day, an otiose observance: pedestrians' pale winter flesh now revealed in the warm weather of near-summer. He shifts in his chair, his point of view restricted to what he's able to see on the other side of the pane.

◊

Up the stairs with a box of bottles and then one final heft into the kitchen, a wobble in her knees. Lily huffs. She's bought whisky and wine. There are snacks on hand. Nineteen booksellers soon to arrive, their annual May party hosted this year by Sachs. And her. She has her breath back. Gives the apartment the once-over: there's ants in the pantry, dust bunnies, bread crumbs between the sofa cushions. Lily shrugs and empties a bag of potato chips into a bowl. Alice bolts from nowhere into her lap. They share a handful. The cat licks her chops.

The apartment clogged with bodies. It's hard to hear, modicums of wit lost to noise and gesture. One unused glass sits on the sloppy kitchen counter. An editor from New Canadian Press cracks a walnut, while Millard John, all nostril and cilia, boasts about a cache of Bloomsbury letters. Lily, arms folded in front of her breasts, nods. Twice she's inverted the man's name. Acorn and MacEwen arrive uninvited. A glass breaks. Alice hides under the bed. Lily needs to refresh her drink.

Excuse me, she says.

MacEwen and Acorn leave. Somebody asks for ice. Sachs hip-to-hip with Betty Porterfield, co-owner of Hoskin Bookseller. She gabs, two drinks in, about her hot find: a *Thin Man* with the word 'erection' on page 138. It caused *such* a scandal, she says. Can you believe it? Knopf tried to pulp the entire first run. This is rare, baby, rare.

Sachs goes to look for Lily. Excuse me, he says.

Davy Goyen, fusty, musty, collects first-edition Surrealists. He sparks some cheap Mexican hay. Others gather. They beat their gums and smoke the stick down.

Sunday morning on the sofa. Lily reads the first line: *After slapping Alexei Tolstoy in the face, M. immediately left for Moscow.* Her left thumb taps the page. She reads the sentence again. Tap tap. Her cuticle picked raw, fresh habit developed this past week. She flips back to the author photo opposite the title page: Nadja Mandelstam, wife of the martyred Osip. She titled her memoir *Hope Against Hope*, a pun on the English translation of her given name, Nadezhda. The poet's wife has worry lines on her forehead, tired eyes, and lips that look like they smirk under pressure. Lily rubs her lunula: the notion that a woman's future could tear from the past, like a hangnail.

Sachs gets off the phone. Well, he says, she's on her way.

No one speaks while the adding machine clacks. There are shared glances from the siblings, an eyeball shorthand that Lily deciphers without trouble. She's ass-cheek on the kitchen counter. She wears a worn denim shirt. His.

At the table, Sachs slouches. Min punches the final button. Through half-rims, she peeks. It's shaping up to be another net loss this year, she says.

Lily saunters to the fridge and pops open an early-afternoon Molson. The sound of the fizz leaves the sister, no doubt, discomfited.

What next?

What *what next*? There is no next. Sell more books. Buy less? Keep inventory lower.

We're known, says Sachs, for our selection.

The best in town, says Lily.

Well, that's not what the numbers say.

Lily takes a swig. That's not very helpful, Min.

Min stands up and starts to pack her adding machine, her eraser. There are loose carbons on the floor. She bends down. I have a stake in this, too, she says. Whatever happens to the store affects me.

Aren't you supposed to be a *silent* partner?

Min takes it on the chin, a sharp jab to be sure, but it's Sachs who winces.

◊

There's a noonday drunk beside your bike. He has a rangy face and uncorked opinions. From a double-parked Audi comes Missy E, full blast. You struggle to hear your own soft curses, your bike sticks and unsticks. The drunk belts it out, an imagined mic at his mouth, *I'll shave your chocha...*

He curtsies, asks for a toonie. You have half to offer. With a chinstrap click and a last look at the old bookshop, you hit the pedals. Hand-signal one block north and slide into the left-turn lane. The advance green imminent.

iPhones Unlocked! Vegan Burritos! The blink of storefront signs as you barrel along. Alert amid the bustle of College Street, mildly adrenal. A cabbie picks up a fare and pulls away from the curb. You have plenty of time to brake. There's a hunched old woman with a handcart, marooned on the traffic island; her demented chortle greets the streetcar riders as they deboard. An old couple holding hands. A gaggle of high schoolers, their anatomy of headphones and sneakers. Some Bluetoothed bozo tries to skirt the crowd and snags her high heel on the tracks. She falls, yelps. No one helps.

The cyclist ahead runs the red. You stop. Pedestrian phalanx in all directions. There's a ghost bike on your right, chained to a post and ring. More and more of these around town, the junked three-speeds painted white and repurposed as roadside memorials to riders killed by cars. This one festooned with azaleas and ribbon. You check the time on your phone even though the clocktower on the Bellevue fire hall stands tall above the intersection. They are three minutes apart.

◊

The credenza, yes. No. No. In *cherry.* Do you have the one in cherry? Uh-huh. The seventy-two-inch? Good. Add that. What's the total now? Goodness. The cost of remodelling. Oh well. Now, about those end tables.

Phoebe hangs up the phone. Flashes Lily a wicked grin. The pair of them found a creative approach to civil disobedience, guerrilla tactics applied with apt metaphor: the plan is to bung up Eaton's warehouse with its own cheap commercial shit. They take turns with the order department. In palaver of the bourgeoisie, they have ridiculous amounts of furniture sent to incorrect addresses. The recipients are all proponents of the expressway. Unwanted shipments will be returned, inventory scrambled. The company will be kicked right in the bottom line.

Now, Lily. She takes a deep breath, dials, and, in a voice that swirls martinis, asks for the most expensive bedroom set to be sent to the home of Mayor Dennison.

◊

Memory of a week ago: the darkness of the room, of the womb, and we were all awake. The baby kicked. Es sighed.

The kid's got your sleeping habits, she said.

Before bed, we had read that dopamine and melatonin flow from the placenta to the still-developing brain. So even without a peep of natural light, the unborn child would learn the difference between night and day.

The opposite, however, seemed to be true: the baby slept when Es was up and about, her steps a soporific. And when she lay down, nothing but a ruckus in her uterus.

Keep it down in there, you said to her stomach.

And – surprise! – there was stillness.

How odd that unborn ears can recognize your voice, that the vibrations of air you create can hit the cochlea, the auditory cortex, but stay free from semantics. Your child attuned not to *what* you say, but *how*.

◊

He rings up three customers in a row. Four more with wallets ready. There's a welcome patter in the shop, marginal commerce. Despite deep sacral protestation, Sachs at last emptied out the backroom. He's ready to reduce stock. A weekend sale moves a lot of books. Friday-night strollers drop by and open their wallets. So, too, the students of philosophy and literature, with long reading lists and short supplies of cash. He jaws with a local poet whose name he never remembers. The cash drawer opens and closes, opens and closes. Lily works the floor and sells all three copies of *The Silent Spring*. A fat Atget. *Organization Man* in both hard and soft cover. At the end of Friday evening, there are vacancies on every shelf. Sachs nods to Lily and turns out the lights. In the darkness, dust motes float.

Night droops onto the rooftops of the city. The moon wanes and drops a weak oblong of light against the living room window. Alice is a shadow across the floor, through a door. She hurtles herself bedward and lands, claws out.

Ow! Shit!

What?

Lily rolls off Sachs. He sits up. His dick already soft. He flicks on the lamp and inspects the cat scratches high on his ankle.

Shit, he says again. Alice curls up beside him and purrs.

Saturday morning, they open ten minutes late. There is a pair already at the door: Mrs. Mintz, dying to haggle, and a lit prof with a taste for the outré. Lily, in denim dress with white stitching, greets him by name: Dr. Gleeman. He checks her out, then the Célines, the Genets. An unfamiliar customer plops a copy of *Topaz* onto the counter. There is a smudge on the bottom corner of the dust jacket.

I should get a discount.

It's already half-price, Sachs says.

The customer's facial features are scrunched between forehead and jaw, a putrid physiognomy. He sniffs. Stomps out. The shop door does not slam; it drifts. Sachs takes the

Uris and starts to daub the cover with rubbing alcohol. He gets the ball game on the radio: *so, there's two balls on Fraser and here's the pitch...*

Pammy DaSilva, Lily's former student, comes in for *No Mean City*, Eric Arthur's paean to demolished history. She flips page after page after page, her first encounter with the lost pilasters of downtown, the turrets, keystones. Sachs reads the girl who reads about those architectural details now dust.

And that's hit deep, deep, but...foul.

Betty Porterfield drops by to snag something good. There's a wastrel in army surplus, lost in whodunits. A blue-haired type buys everything in Natural History; she wants to charge $86.43 to her card, but it's cash only so her actual purchase is less than half. Sachs carries three heavy shopping bags to her car and returns to find Phoebe whispering something to Lily. Their initial guffaw restrained at his approach.

What's so funny?

Nothing, says Phoebe. She wipes a tear from her eye.

Lily clears her throat. Okay if I cut out early?

Simultaneous nod and shrug from Sachs. The women wave and cut across Spadina. He watches them go. Something in their cadence, a drift he cannot catch. Unobserved, the wastrel makes off with four mysteries, unpaid.

Lily and Phoebe hit the Coffee Mill, a patio courtyard off Bloor. The owner, von Heczey, greets them as regulars and offers a corner table. Chatter all around, a swirl of conversations both raucous and discreet. Phoebe tops up their mugs with something from a flask. They clink and drink, two purveyors of radical politics who take the time to discuss concerns both amatory and monetary.

You're not kidding? says Lily. You really fucked Vern?

What can I say, says Phoebe, I'm just a foot soldier in the sexual revolution.

Lily snorts.

Plus, Blatnyck canned me.

What? When? Did he give a reason?

Phoebe sips. Last week. No reason. Too many typos maybe? No more handjobs? The point is: my bank account's in the toilet.

Geez, Pheeb.

And then Vern got evicted. Again. So, you know, it was good timing. He needed a place to crash. I needed some help with the rent.

Geez, Lily says again.

Stop saying that. Didn't you do the same thing? Shacked up when you got fired?

I got suspended. Not fired.

Same diff.

The women pause to watch a bony number take the next table. Floppy red hat, big blue shades. She flips open the front section of the newspaper. Her lips move while she reads.

Lily follows the residue of coffee in her cup. I called my union rep the other day. Did I tell you this?

Un-uh.

There's still some paperwork to be done. A hearing with the trustee and Libov. But he figures I'll be reinstated in time for summer school.

Cool, says Phoebe.

I told him no thanks.

Huh?

I told him I'm not coming back. Said it's time to try something different.

I thought you love teaching.

I do, says Lily. Parts of it. I love the kids, the ones who want to learn, anyway. But all the other bullshit. You know, the *bureaucracy*.

That, my friend, is everywhere.

Lily shrugs. Maybe, she says.

Phoebe checks her watch. Let's go, she says. We're meeting up at five.

◊

You pull an Idaho stop. The side streets are designed to calm traffic — alternate one-ways, chicanes — but a garbage truck is the only vehicle in sight. A worker, burly and tatted, hops off the back and drags a pair of green bins from the curb. The summer scent of organic waste. You weave around him and pass a toothy realtor's crooked sign. The next house has a Little Free Library. You brake for a gander.

Major and Ulster streets, Brunswick Avenue: you obey the one-ways. Never used to. You, the downtown cyclist, dug the careen and dodge. You rode through thunderstorms, you rode in crazy heat. Nowadays, you go easier on the derailleur. Do the gentlest of index shifts. A gawker's cadence: bay-and-gables still catch your eye, no matter how many times you've pedalled past. The dilapidated ones stand out – drooped and peeled, with cracked brick that surrounds carved-sunburst corbels. You break for a stroller. Father and daughter toe-dip in the Fairley Park wading pool. Named for Margaret Fairley, the old Coleridge scholar and activist; Coleridge the Romantic and addict, who wrote that the difference between genius and talent is like the disparity between the egg and the eggshell.

◊

Can't we wait somewhere else?

Why?

This guy, says Vern Dyson, he keeps checking me out.

Phoebe's eye is less than covert. Him? she says. The guy in the white hot pants? He's kinda cute.

Give me a break.

They play pinball in the St. Charles Tavern. The beer is flat. The lights, even late afternoon, are turned low. Two men sway to Peggy Lee's 'Fever,' while Lily, on a pay phone beside the can, gets the lowdown from Irving: their wheels have fallen through.

A bum fan belt, Lily says to the others, but he thinks they can finagle another.

Whose?

Irv knows a guy.

Shit, says Vern. He sucks his teeth.

Be cool, man.

Lily leans against the machine, where the words *Shoot Again* blink against the backglass.

Got ourselves a free game, Phoebe says.

Looks like it.

The tide's changing.

Turning.

Huh?

The tide turns, says Lily. Times change.

Phoebe fires the plunger. You said it, sister.

Dinnertime, uptown. A creamy Ford, plateless and dented, slows where Coldstream Avenue meets Glengrove. The spot is away from the street lights, out of the sightlines of middle-class windows. Claude cuts the ignition and the crew gets out. Vern Dyson carries a cardboard box filled with seed bombs. Lily's the first one to reach in, the ball of sun-baked potter's clay a perfect fit for her hand. She stands in front of the eight-foot-high security barrier. The big ditch is on the other side. Scrub and pebble and, at the bottom, the half-built Eglinton expressway exit. She gauges height and distance and hurls the bomb. No explosion, but a healthy scatter of ovules. Her resistance to car culture comes with the hopeful future of germination.

What kind of seeds did you use? says Irving. He lobs one that hits the top of the fence and bounces back.

Sunflower seeds, mostly. Some cosmos. Hollyhock.

Phoebe whips one. Her arc is high and true.

You've got a good arm.

Ready for the big leagues.

Everyone rears back and fires. As the box empties, the sun begins to set. The sky takes on a cooler hue.

He stews under a lavender sky. Much foot-shuffling in this shade. It's a long line outside the Imperial Theatre and he's at the back, eyes out for her arrival. She will not make it. Sachs casts a sustained look at the box, at the napes and collars of the unticketed. This night is the final showing of *A New Leaf*.

Lily arrives and kisses him on the cheek. Sorry I'm late, she says.

I hate missing the credits.

She springs for popcorn. They share the bag without a touch of each's buttered fingers. In the dark, on the screen, Matthau struggles to untangle May from her Grecian nightgown.

◊

Small irritations that go unmentioned. Clarifications formed in silence and stranded there. This is how the end begins. Neither Sachs nor Lily are inarticulate people and yet the

— 88 —

locution of each gets sapped the longer they are together. Their first two months, even the third, were voluble and erogenous. The sex remained reciprocal for the fourth. Fifth, Sachs holds his tongue more and more, his touch saturnine. He now fucks like a husband.

◊

It's a steady creaking shuffle he hears, one floor above. A copy of *Going Places* in his lap. He listens to the mind that wanders from windowsill to closet to kitchen counter: she can never find her keys. Sachs sighs, his chair creaks. A silverfish creeps out of the book's gutter.

He flips the shop sign from *Open* to *Closed* and waits, fists in pockets, while Lily comes down.

You coming or not?

Un-huh, he says.

The Association needs you.

The Spadina Businessmen's Association? What on earth do they need from me?

Solidarity. The security of a unified front.

I signed the petition. I signed a dozen petitions.

I just wish you'd be more involved.

In my own way, I am. The shop is the street, right? Like Jane Jacobs says.

Fuck Jane Jacobs. I'm not talking about just sitting around. I'm talking about being an active, engaged citizen.

She reaches out. Fingers on her right hand circle his wrist and tug with gentle intent. His gaze floats to a pair of pale freckles along her ulna. He studies them without augury.

The lounge flashes neon and chrome. The drapes are pink, same as the leather stool covers. The Silver Rail touts its high tails, its flips and sours, but the guys both have whisky, straight.

Where's Lily tonight? says Joe.

Giving a speech, says Sachs, to the Spadina Businessmen's Association.

Why aren't you there? You're a Spadina businessman.

I already got the speech.

The bar is long and has such high polish he can see fragments of reflection, his outlined mug. Joe looks elsewhere. The fight on TV: Bad Bennie Briscoe lands a big right to some unranked schlub, a bleeder whose record will take a hit before the third bell.

I saw Briscoe once, says Joe. Three, four years back. In Philly. He KO'd Red Top Owens in the sixth.

Sachs signals for two more.

Sheesh. When'd you become such a boozer?

When'd you become such a lightweight?

Heh. Reminds me of this joke, says Joe. This old Yid sits at the bar. Real quiet. Sips his drink. And then this loudmouth shows up, a bruiser, real Aryan type, and he sneers at the old guy and buys a round for everyone − except, he says, *for this dumb Jew*. The old guy shrugs: whatever. Next night, same thing. A round for everyone. Except the dumb Jew. Every night for a week. Rounds for everyone. And then finally he can't help himself. He says: What's with you, Hebe? You too dumb to take the hint. And the old guy says, Nope...

Sachs interrupts with a raised forefinger. *'I'm the owner,'* he says.

Oh, says Joe. You know that one.

◊

West on the Harbord bike lane. You're wheel to wheel. In front, a fixed-gear dude with a bottleneck ajut out of his leather courier bag. And behind, a college girl with blue rinse and plastic daisies entwined in her wire basket. An e-bike toodles between you and an SUV.

◊

Five figures in a moonless parking lot. They leave no shadow as they take their positions at the north doors of Eaton's department store. Vern Dyson looks in every direction.

You sure there's no security here?

Sure I'm sure, says Irving. We've already scoped it out. This'll be a snap. Claude?

Claude unzips a duffle bag and pulls out a pair of caulking guns. He loads a ten-ounce tube in each and hands one to his boyfriend. Irving squeezes the trigger. Gunk covers the door hinges and the jamb. The door is now stuck in its frame.

It'll solidify in a minute or two, he says.

Ha! Good luck opening *that* this morning.

Eat it, Yorkdale!

Phoebe takes a step closer. Lemme try the next one.

There are five doors in each set, seven more sets around the entire mall. Lily does the last, the expressway's cloverleaf exchange in the distance behind her. The nighttime air is damp, her palms sweaty. At the same moment, downtown, Sachs wakes to find her pillow is still cool.

All next day, a heaviness in the air. The sky in shades more and more grey – granite, slate, shale – and then with a boom not unexpected the rain comes, the sort of hard summer rain that drops the mercury and clears the sinuses. Lily opens the window. Drops of water pound the sill. Alice on the sofa stretches, sniffs, resettles. On the floor, Sachs again rearranges his tiles. There's a double-letter square that he can reach via an upward column. He has a Q, but no U. He searches for an acceptable combination. *QTBVIMJ*. Scrabble is not his game; his interest lies in pure lexicon rather than strategy. Lily does not move. Her eyes adjust to the speed of rain.

Hey, says Sachs at last. Is *tivy* a word?

◊

Hope and Grubb take turns at the podium. Nomenclature notwithstanding, they manage to agree on one single fact: the city cannot approach its future until the province hands down the final decision on the expressway.

Hope: Whatever happens next, it will be neither an ending nor a beginning. Our communities will always be in flux. What matters is that we have found our voice. We have learned how to speak as one.

And then Grubb: It's fair to say our operation is on hold. We have no firm plans yet. But the reality is that we are a development company. Our main concern is land. We will continue to pick up options. We will continue to buy properties.

Next, the Q&A: querulous, antagonistic. A Willowdale lawyer carps about his commute and gets shouted down by a quartet of angry ratepayers. Junction hard hats, desperate for work, cuss and boo. The Metro comptroller adjusts his figures, reporters from the *Globe* and *Telegram* and *Star* scribble with haste. Someone scrooches, someone elbows. The gym at Lord Lansdowne P.S. is full and hot and now comes the moment when oxygen turns fugitive: Grubb signals for an egress. His bruiser steps in, a deviated-septum sort in an ill-fitted suit. A holster spotted in his jacket gap. A worried buzz makes its way and finds Phoebe, who whispers to Lily, who alerts a nearby community police officer and, after another quiet word, the thug is frisked. He's licensed; Lily's incensed. She kicks the goon in the balls. A loud groan and several shoves and the cop arrests the only person within reach.

With no money to cover bail, Sachs has no choice but to drop a dime. He holds the handset loosely, then with a more insistent grip. He dials, hears mild static on the line after he hits up Joe for a loan.

What? he says.

I didn't say anything, says Joe.

That's a first.

Way to butter me up.

Can you front me the dough, Joe? You know I'm good for it.

Yeah, but is she?

I thought you liked her.

Buddy, I hate to say this. But: she's taking you for a ride.

Well, says Sachs, you managed to say that without much difficulty.

You're paying her rent.

Joe.

Now you're paying her bail.

Joe!

Yeah?

Will you lend it to me or not?

Not three hours later, Sachs gets Lily out of the cooler. She remains, however, hot under the collar.

A gun? What kind of creep brings a gun to a community meeting?

She crumples her bail ticket and tosses it toward the trash, but the wad of paper hits the lip of the basket and tumbles onto the sidewalk in front of 51 Division.

Sachs is half a step behind her. First it's public distur-
bance, he says in a voice nowhere near light enough. Now
it's littering. What's your next crime going to be?

◊

Three blocks of Palmerston. Light speckles through leaves
of silver maples. A row of nineteenth-century street lamps,
their original glass globes recently replaced with polycar-
bonate ones. An old stone gate post at the end of the street.
This was once a tony boulevard, an address for mayors and
grocery barons, but the gentry departed and a new generation
of landlords halved, quartered, eighthed the homes. For
decades, wage earners and students moved in. Now the flats
and bachelors and rooms are being reconverted, the heavy
oak doors open again for the affluent and the splurgers.

You hesitate at the yellow light and have to brake at the red.

North of Bloor, brief contravention of a one-way, then you
take the lane on the left. On your right, the Palmerston
Library. Where, eleven years ago, you came in to pay overdue
fines on a *Planet Earth* DVD. This was before streaming, before
sexting. Behind the desk was Es. You had spoken only the
barest pleasantries prior to this, but enthusiasm for the Birds
of Paradise gave her voice.

Such gorgeous plumage, she said.

You fumbled your loonies. You had a wine stain on your white tee.

She scanned your card and up came the record of your patronage: name and address and the books you had checked out. What else did you have, back then, by way of definition? Es grew pinkish in the cheeks. She likes to say you were an easy read. Even at first blush.

Then came the second set of keys, and then a bigger bed. Double to a king, enough space to keep her out of range of your midnight restlessness. Before you knew it, a box on your tax return was marked *common law*. Breakfast and dinner with Es, thousands of times over. Make no mistake: this was the life you had always imagined. The fatherless narrative, the enduring present. It lasted for a decade.

After that, it went back and forth. To have a child or not. The actual decision was far less momentous than what ensued: amniocentesis, sonograms, a tempo adjusted at your first parenting class. The teacher's name was Leonora. She wore a *Bikini Kill* tee and schoolmarm glasses. Her cv listed obstetric nurse, midwife, lactation consultant. She had all the answers for parents-to-be. Save one.

Why can't you keep the rhythm? she said to you.

Reggae, she had just told us, has the right bouncy cadence to rock newborns to sleep. 'No Woman, No Cry' played from her phone. Each future father cradled a baby doll and slowly circled the room; all but you maintained 4/4 time. Around and around you went, your feet unable to find the skanky beat. You can still hear maternal titters, Marley's semi-rhoticity, his unstressed syllables.

◊

The 7 bus chugs up the Davenport hill. The incline a steep reminder of the prehistoric lake that receded from here and so sculpted the municipal terrain: shore bluff, creek, and ravine. The city shaped by ancient absence.

Red light at the apex. Pedestrians cross. Three more passengers get on board, one an aged schmo with a walker. Sachs offers his seat.

All I'm saying, he says, is don't tell her about your arrest.

Don't tell me what to tell her.

Sorry. Just, I know how she'll react. The whole visit will be strained.

Lily withholds her response. She pouts in contemplation. He hangs on a strap. Bathurst Street is all ups and downs. The road climbs and then straightens over the Cedarvale Ravine and the row of luxury apartments, circa 1920, low-rised and Deco-detailed. The bus speeds past a pair of syna-gogues, makes the light at Eglinton, and rides the strip-plaza gullet north of Lawrence, where Sachs gives a tentative yank on the stop-request cord.

The stink of charcoal and stogie. A fleck of tobacco on Larry's tongue yet he continues to gas on about a missing shipment of carburetors.

And now they can't find the invoice! Can you believe that? I've been doing business with Artie Dunkleman for what? eight, nine years? This isn't the first time he's screwed up. What am I going to do? My customers are waiting.

Sachs flicks Lily a look. She sits in the grass, her back turned to him. An oppugnant tilt to her shoulders. He looks the other way and sees Aitch pick a blade of grass, a blade, another blade.

He's in one of his moods again, Min says. She flips the dogs. Moves them from grill to platter and carries the whole shebang, buns and all, to the picnic table positioned in the backyard's shadiest spot.

Two minutes in the sun and the kid's a pastrami, says Larry. Me, I love it. I end up looking like a *schwartze*.

Larry! says Min.

What?

We don't say that anymore.

Listen, they say much worse about us.

Sachs squeezes the relish. He's heard it all before: his sister and her gnattish suggestions, her husband's nattered rejoinders. The social niceties of their class erode more and more until Lily notices Aitch's absence and the gate swinging wide open.

What the?

Easy, take it easy.

Where'd?

Can't be far.

Min, on the front porch, stands lookout. The others split up: east to a nearby park, south behind a neighbour's bush, west around the corner, where Sachs comes across an abandoned shoe and sock. He follows the clues: the second shoe, a mustard-stained tee. Shorts. Underwear. He closes in on the little nudist.

He found *you.* Your mother always colours this story with unequal daubs of humour and concern. But what could have happened? You had tried to escape into a cul-de-sac. Where else could you have gone?

He found you. And you have not been able to return the favour. You have teased out every tiny moment, considered all the evidence. He remains the family ellipsis, a middle-aged simulacrum insulated from the jolt of reality you are only now ready to accept.

◊

The city on edge. There has been no news from the premier's office. Nothing but speculation from the city hall beat, the trio of local papers circulate rumour both more and less credible. J. J. Robinette appears on camera, somehow both long-winded and mum. Blatnyck has no inklings. Lily says little. In this absence, Joe's opinions gain fresh solidity:

This town has two speeds. Slow and slower. Eventually, we'll have to catch up to the present.

Sachs pounds the pocket of his mitt. Just throw the ball, he says.

Joe throws.

Sachs catches. They start with a short toss. Then, once their arms are stretched out, they take a step back, another, until the distance is covered with just enough effort.

Think about it, says Joe. What happens if the province says no? We never get to make our own decisions. We never get to grow up.

Nnff, says Sachs. He moves to his left and nabs a one-hopper. Over cocktails at a semi-detached on Robert Street, some STOP side jock pitched a friendly softball game: Huron-Sussex ratepayers versus the Spadina Businessmen. Just a little levity while everyone waits on the big decision, just a little fun. Sachs cajoled into it. He hasn't picked up his glove in years, so time for a little practice before game day. He scoops a grounder. Fires. Joe fires back. The throw is errant, wide, and high so Sachs backpedals. Over his shoulder, he gets a bead on it. The ball, at perihelion, begins to descend.

Pretty good wheels, says Joe, for an old guy.

Another late night with no word from her. Sachs adoze on the sofa, book open on his chest. The gentle rise and fall disturbed by a knock, knock, knock. His lids twitch. KNOCK. And he's on his feet, cautious down the darkened stairs, even more cautious as he gets closer to the knuckle

rap on the other side of the door. He opens it a crack, alde-
hyde breath.

Shorry, says Lily. Losht my keysh.

He goes back up the stairs, but this time with a sinking
feeling.

A little worse for wear the next morning. Lily takes her time.
A long shower, then a short stroll to the Crescent Grill, where
she scarfs lipids and gathers enough oomph for an afternoon
visit to the nursing home. She is, of course, gentle in her
ministrations, though a strain in mind leaves her slightly absent.

Your hair used to be so black, Gram. Remember? So glossy.

Ida's pupils are dark furious dots. The hairbrush is heavy
with a solid pewter handle. It belonged to Lily's great-
grandmother, who passed it on to her grandmother, who has
used it for both grooming and as a gavel: so many table-
smackings over so many years. In Lily's hands, the family
heirloom is far less dramatic. She brushes her grandmother's
hair. One long firm stroke after another, scalp to ends, and
then she pauses to see what is tangled in the bristles.

◊

He kills the afternoon at the laundromat. Loads the dryer.
Presses the start button and quickly gets caught in a staring
contest with a commercial Kenmore. Fragments of reflection

imposed on the flip-flop of clothes. He sees flecks of his grey hair and her denim skirt, bra strap, and eyes that refuse to blink. Unwavering in the face of his face. Nothing in this visage suggests decorum. He will regret what he does do and what he doesn't. He leans forward. Looks closer. Clothes tangle and untangle before him. Regret, reflect, reject. It all goes around and around.

Just past ten p.m. She sits there, underwear around her ankles while Sachs brushes his teeth. He's shirtless and she follows the familiar route of follicle and mole. Six months of ablutions have washed away the erotic. She watches splotches of paste hit the medicine-cabinet mirror and searches for that one tacit moment, well back, when their touch became about utility. He rinses and spits. Lily grabs paper off the roll, wipes and flushes.

This is the last time they have sex. Such a sweatless finality. She smokes a joint just to get in the mood. The affair continues to dwindle. He is not without knowledge, pinpricks of certainty down his shoulders and spine. He arranges himself on the bed. In situations like these, the most important thing is to come first.

◊

Blatnyck's office, Sunday afternoon. Workday cigarette smoke sticks around weekends and answers, perhaps, for the sallowness of a potted fern. A diploma from Queen's on the wall, the usual sheepskin font with the school's official seal and the dean's indecipherable signature. Lily fiddles with a thick rubber band. Stretches it between thumb and forefinger. She stops, looks at her feet, resumes her fidget.

It's not B and E, technically, says Phoebe. I still have keys.

She pulls open a filing cabinet drawer and flips through folders of clients recently busted: possession, burglary tools; possession, firearms; possession, narcotics – that's a fat one: possession, stolen property. She searches for the name of a reliable crook.

Trespassing, then.

Phoebe slaps a page. Whatever, she says. You sure you want to do this?

Lily nods. I'm sure.

Okay. Let's give this guy a call.

They wait in the shadeless plaza of the Toronto-Dominion banking pavillion. Two dark towers, constructed of black steel and bronze-tinted glass, adhere to the rigid mathematics of space at the corner of King and Bay Streets. Mies van der Rohe's windswept modernism is the perfect place to hock goods. No one hangs out here after business hours.

Phoebe points. Here he comes.

Franco, in a woven Trilby and curlicue of smoke, approaches. He nods. His hat is the colour of a nicotine stain.

Ladies, he says.

Phoebe nudges Lily. No pleasantries are on offer. Her fist opens and there's a pendant and a ring in her palm. Both sapphire, both smuggled by a great-uncle out of Kielce three generations ago. Uncaptured during a pogrom, but there is no escape from penury.

How much? says Lily.

Depends.

On?

On your story.

My story? says Lily. What happened to *no questions asked*?

Franco flicks away his cigarette and inspects the dangler, the bluish gem reflecting distant light.

Straight skinny, sister. Where'd you get such hot rocks?

They're not stolen.

No-o-o-o.

They're not. They're mine. They've been passed down in my family.

Franco grabs his crotch. Family jewels, eh? I can dig.

C'mon, Julian.

It's pronounced *Hoo-li-an*.

Sorry.

De nada. Sixty bucks.

For the pendant?

For everything.

Hundred.

Seventy.

Ninety.

Eighty, he says. Take it or leave it.

Sachs is halfway down the stairs, a Rogin in hand, when Lily appears at the bottom. He stops. So does she, sclerotic seconds before she pulls the four twenties out of her pocket.

What's that?

Money I owe you. The bail.

You don't need to pay me back, Lil. You can work it off. You *have* been working it off.

Get real, please. You don't need me there. You barely need *you* there.

Sachs nudges his right shoe to the edge of the riser. What does that mean? he says.

Nothing, says Lily. Sorry.

She takes three steps up. He comes down one. You mean business is slow.

I mean, maybe, it might not get any better. Maybe you need to, y'know, think about what happens next.

Sachs descends again, a brief pause while he shares Lily's stair before he squeezes past.

Maybe, he says.

◊

Game day, at Christie Pits park. Sachs takes strike three. He grabs some bench beside Ray Wiggins. Ray, a ringer from Mobile, an ex-shortstop who now washes dishes in the Paramount Tavern.

I played in Drummondville, Quebec. I played in Montreal. I played in Trois-fucking-Rivières.

Uh-huh.

I once hit a dinger off Gentry Jessup, man!

He takes a puff on his Export 'A'. The cig bobs baton-wise, matches the tempo of his down-home dialect. Ever make it with one of those French girls?

Nope.

Ray reaches for his bat. He has powerful forearms and dishpan hands. They're just like English girls, he says. Except when they come, they like to say, *oui, oui, oui.*

Top of the third. The team trots across the line, from foul territory to fair. Sachs stands in the langorous expanse of centre field and yawns. He glances around. There are some spectators on the benches that run parallel to the baseline, but most sit on the grassy slopes high above the diamond. The field, a former sandpit, is well below street level.

Lily is not there.

He works his glove with jangly impatience and when the ball is socked, finally, after seven interminable innings, he lopes after it without dubiety. A pop-up betwen centre and short. Achy hamstrings loosen. A leatherlungs exhorts. He runs and runs, trailing the trajectory of the high fly. He reaches for it, reaches, and then – BONK! – he crashes into Ray. An elbow, a temple. Sachs hits the grass, the ball rolls out of his glove dizzily, like the lone survivor of a three-car pileup.

◇

You ride on: smooching teenagers in a parkette, KFC stink. You speed away from eleven herbs and spices, up a potholed laneway with Day-Glo graffiti on every second garage door: *R.I.P. Shi Boi. I EAT DICK.* Skill-saw whine, sports talk radio. So receptive to your familiar route, you pedal, ocular, olfactive. Out onto Barton Avenue now. Five minutes from home. There's sweat under your chinstrap as you get nearer to Christie – the street, after the completion of Spadina, that would have been demolished for another expressway. The light turns yellow, ball field at the Pits in sight. You really push it. You're almost at the intersection when a Prius driver opens his door and you brake, bomp, and go ass-over-handlebar.

Sorry, sorry, I'm sorry.

Uhn.

I'm so sorry. I'm a cyclist, too. Y'know. I didn't, I really…

Urf, you say. You sit up. You're in the middle of the road. You have all your teeth.

The driver is on his knees, ID spills across his quads. Driver's licence, membership card from an insurance company. You catch sight of his shopping list. He needs mangos.

There are pieces of reflector all around. Your bell not just rung. Shattered. Clamp and rivet roll toward the sidewalk. You make a cud-chewing motion to loosen your jaw.

I'm all right. I live right nearby.

Lemme call 911. I'm so...

I'm okay. Really. I just want to go home.

◊

This is where he becomes lost in your thoughts, a terra incognita. Footfalls in your temporal lobe, each one uncertain. Let's say he walks off the field, up the hill, and out of the Pits. Float your eyes over the intersection. A bus passes. He stands there. His temple throbs down to this toes. There are many steps still to take. Hundreds, in fact; the sun is glarier in this stride, the horns honkier. Ankle ligaments have a weak synaptic snap. In a wonky reverse of the route you just made, Sachs, concussed, cannot shrug off what comes next. A whack on the head is one thing, a whomp to the chest is another.

Here it comes.

He makes it back home. Lily is waiting. They stand at arm's length from each other. She looks at her feet, takes a discreet half-step back. The rug needs a vaccum. A bulb in the lamp has burned out. Alice sits on the sill of the open window, far more engaged in minor activities outside than the muggy language stuffed inside.

Hal, says Lily.

The cat, all of a sudden, is on all fours. Lean and low, a hunter's crouch. She has spotted something, something that leaves her appetent and keen. Chirrups and Alice's low throaty chatter ignored by the two people in earshot. There are stacks of books on the landing, in the limbo between being read for pleasure and being priced for sale. There's a half-eaten pizza in a box and paper towels, crumpled and greasy, on the table. No one says anything, but somehow there's a reverb of all the words unspoken. Lily stands still, straight, emphatic as an exclamation point.

Hal, she says again.

And then Alice leaps out the window.

Sachs and Lily clunk heads. Both of them peer over the ledge. No sight of her. How far could she have gone? And how fast? They take the stairs two, three, four at a time and are in a sidewalk muddle of drunks, seamstresses, and noodle-shop workers on smoke break. Sachs asks a *Sing Tao* seller. Lily checks an alley. The horizon line is pink and smoggy as the first seconds of night settle in.

They split up. Cover twice the ground in half the time. Still, this takes hours. Sachs up and down Augusta, Kensington. The fruit stands and poultry butchers are closed, so he has few inquiries to make. Pops his head into an after-hours joint, where old Portuguese men play dominoes and discuss Salazar's most recent demagoguery. No one has seen anything.

Lily knocks on doors and asks permission to investigate front and backyards. There are alleys behind restaurants with a hundred possible nooks, but all she finds is rubbish and food-scrap rats and the initial whiff of resignation.

Overnight, Spadina Avenue has grown too wide. There are too many pedestrians, the terrible expanse filled with opportunity for accident and malfeasance. Every sidestep, every horn honk leaves Lily braced for bad news. She has woken Phoebe up early and the pair flour-pastes one telephone pole after another: *Missing, Missing, Missing.* They have been out all day, searched every which way. Put posters in the windows of delis and jobbers'. Waitress in a Szechuan place shakes her head. They open cans of tuna and wait in doorways, but this only attracts strays, mottled and scabby and ear-bitten. Lily sits down, removes her right sandal, and massages the ball of the foot. Her nose is sunburned.

Forget it, she says. It's over.

Don't say that, says Phoebe. We'll find her.

That's not what I meant.

Oh.

Can I stay at your place tonight?

Um. Okay.

There's a pay phone at the corner. A dime would be the cheapest breakup ever. She almost stops, but forces herself farther up the block. She walks without apparent weariness, though, in truth, she is already so overwhelmed by the need for respite that she starts to yawn outside the bookshop. Sachs, of course, is inside; there's no one else. The moment will never be better. The moment will never be right. Lily struggles to speak, palate and tongue are jammed, and when the first syllable comes out, it is brittle, uncomfortable, in a voice that is all elbows.

Hal, she says.

She leaves. He remains seated. Browsers come and go. Someone buys something. And then, within the odd confines of reluctance, he is alone in the shop. Him and the books. They speak volumes.

◊

Rundown houses and renos alternate. A pair of schnauzers yip your way. This spate of double vision starts to clear as you limp up Christie. Minutes from home, a good dose of quiddity the closer you get. All these years of riding in this city and you can, finally, celebrate your first door prize. You have three popped spokes. There is something loose in the stem or fork and the handlebar slides parallel with the top tube. You walk your bike and veer, you overcompensate, you veer.

◊

A blade of light slips through the window and stabs him below the left nipple. He flinches. No sleep last night, nothing restful beneath lashes and lids. Sachs pulls on his jeans. Buttons his shirt. Out of habit, he makes coffee for two.

◊

The night spent contorted in a loveseat. An errant spring, a pointed reminder of this shabby pad: empty fridge, full ashtray. In the past six months, she has moved out, moved in with Sachs, moved back. The only change here is who fucks whom. And where. Irving and Claude sleep in her old room.

Yes, Lily says into the receiver. Tabby. One eye. Anything?

She winds the phone cord around her index finger. The Humane Society has had her on hold for eight minutes. Phoebe emerges from her room in a man's pyjama top, fills up a glass of water, and drinks it down. Vern Dyson's drunken snore rattles the floor tiles. A toilet flushes in the apartment next door. The pipes are hidden within thin, half-plastered walls. A gurgle eddies around the response on the other end of the line.

Sorry, says Lily. Can you repeat that?

Her throat muscles go taut, bloodshot eyes start to see everything in red: One eye! Isn't that distinguishing enough?

◊

Sachs starts to pace, then sits. He sits, then starts to pace. *The apartment is quiet as paper.*

◊

Joe Sharpe is on a real run this morning. He takes a call from Grubb and learns another city inspector has been paid off. A questionable eviction has been upheld. He jumps at the chance to change the locks and afterward stops in a menswear store to celebrate with a new tie. Pink-and-green paisley. His mug in the mirror approves. With his wallet out, Joe starts to calculate. He's always been a luck-pusher, the kind of guy who knows when to let it ride. So he sacrifices some shoe leather and figures to make a killing. The last step up Mrs. Mintz's stairs is a jaunty one. He rings the bell.

This is very sensitive information, he says.

They recline on chintz cushions. He implies secret knowledge, takes the old bird into his suspect confidence.

I've got the ear of an alderman — I can't say who — but let's just say I've got new assurances. This deal is going through, Mrs. Mintz. If you ask me, there'll never be a better time to sell.

Mrs. Mintz nibbles a sugar cookie. A chunk crumbles toward the carpet.

Ten minutes later, he is back on the sidewalk. He whistles 'Moonlight Serenade,' the air light and aloft from his lips until a throaty mewl provides a surprise counterpoint. There's a paw on his trousers. Joe glances down.

Meeorrw, says Alice the cat.

◊

The shop stays closed. In front of the unlit shelves, Sachs stands. Surrounded by a billion words – typeset, printed, bound – and yet not a single one, nor any combination, can help him encapsulate this certain instinct. Down the familiar aisle he goes and with an inward humour puts up the sign: *Back in 5 Minutes*. His key is out, the deadbolt passes slyly through the strike plate. Outside, the evening is cool and there are wide-open spaces along the sidewalk. Quick look at the passenger-side window of a parked car, millisecond of a wised-up gaze. There is little traffic on Spadina Avenue. He moves through these early morning hours with a peculiar grace, elides streetwalkers and stoners and nightshifters and passes under lighted windows, the windows of both lovers and insomniacs.

◊

The boys rouse themselves just after noon. Coffee cools off, yet still they speak with bitter tongues.

It's simple, says Irving. A little fertilizer, a wad of cotton. You soak it in diesel fuel, light the fucker, and boom.

Claude smacks the tabletop. BOOM! he says.

Lily's lids are heavy. Her forehead worries.

No one'll get hurt. It'll be the dead of night.

Just gonna blow that hunk of concrete to bits.

The on-ramp?

The *off*-ramp, says Claude. So people can't get *to* the mall.

Lily clears her throat. Her voice is raspy and dangerous, like a struck match. Wanton destruction, she says. It'll rally the other side.

Phoebe is in the shower. A water stain on the north wall spreads like gangrene.

We already voted on this, says Irving. Four to one. He pulls a fresh smoke from a pack. Three clicks on his lighter before the spark and catch.

Besides, Vern's already out buying the manure.

With a deft wiggle of his Slim Jim, Claude pops the lock. He reaches under the dash and connects the red wires. The engine revs. The crew climbs in. An innocuous speed at three a.m. A long stretch of Bathurst is empty, save for a mismatch of cabs and fares. Further uptown, Irving spots a police cruiser parked at a gas station. The headlights are off, a bulky shadow behind the wheel. Claude stays easy on the gas. In the back seat, variations of pulse: Phoebe and Vern Dyson squeeze damp hands. Lily rolls down her window. It's breezeless inside the car, a cool soup. A left turn onto Lawrence Avenue, past a corner plaza. They are not far from Min and Larry's. There is a block of public housing, a block of bungalows, a high school. A burned-out street lamp above, a dark wink, and then, just ahead, the on-ramp. They accelerate. Tire drone beneath the chassis, a rubberized threnody for who-knows-what. Claude takes the Yorkdale cut-off hard and fast. His forearms jolt, the wheels squeal, and all five of them ooch and ugh as the hot Ford exits the expressway. One final screech around the curve of the cloverleaf. The auto smashes through the guardrail and, fenderless and unfix-able, hisses to a halt under the concrete off-ramp. The hood steams. The radicals wobble.

Phew, says Phoebe. That was dramatic.

Irving opens the trunk. Get moving!

With rehearsed precision, they pack fertilizer into paper bags. Douse the cotton in diesel and stuff one homemade bomb beside the gas tank and another in the glove compartment. The blast will shatter everything within five hundred square feet. They have calculated how far they have to run to safety, and how fast.

Claude smooches Irving. Let's do it.

Irving flicks his lighter. Nothing. Again and again. He whips it away. The others frisk themselves. No one has anything.

Lily, with relaxed and unculpable hands, takes a minute to study the three-starred sky. Well, she says. This is just stupid.

◊

For chrissakes, says Larry, He's a grown man. Maybe he doesn't want to talk to his sister every day.

What every day? What's wrong with once a week?

Min long ago had learned to fake certain kinds of accep-tance: her husband's distaste for leftovers, the way her brother was tardy with his return calls. Sure, she might fill the tape in his answering machine, but it was always with a casual air. She could wait. She could listen to the dial tone without portent. She could also grab his spare keys and drive down there. Traffic is bad. Road repair south of Glencairn accelerates her nerves and for the first time in her life she exceeds the speed limit. Her radio is on:

If we are building a transportation system to serve the automobile, Premier William Davis says to the Provincial Legislature on June 3, 1971, *the Spadina Expressway would be a good place to start. But if we are building a transportation system to serve people, the Spadina Expressway is a good place to stop.*

Lily is on the street when word gets out. A teamster she knows, through a mouthful of onion bun, schmecks something that sounds like *topple.*

What?

The teamster's second try is purple-faced. He horks and chokes. Five hard backslaps from Lily force the troublesome wad of dough from windpipe to sidewalk.

They – stopped – it.

Spadina Avenue, from this moment, becomes bloated with detail: over the airwaves, across the countertops, off the tongues of professors and furriers. The afternoon editions are soon unbundled and beneath twelve-point type are black-and-white jubilations and teeth-grit quotes. Mayor Dennison, on city business in Ceprano, expresses his utter disbelief. Some are on record assuring the death of civic autonomy, others the birth of a responsive government. Nowhere does the news resound more than in the half-empty shelves of Cecil Street Books, the darkened display window. The indecision that unwavered there, the inability to take a step forward. It's all up for grabs now. The stock will be sold off. The lease will be broken. There will be no payoff.

◊

Try to reimagine him, maybe somewhere warm. Dawn-dappled sweetgum, a dusty road. He hitches a ride with an apple-cheeked nun. She offers him a Kool. Sachs closes his eyes, his head still hurts from the blow to his temple. The drive through Texas is lulling. Abeline, Big Spring. He is unshaven, without a book in his pocket. Gets dropped off just outside of Sanderson, where he paces well into the night, the dark motel lot occasionally aglow with the streaking red lights of intercontinental rigs.

◊

Twenty-three years of plans made and amended. Seventy-five million dollars spent, with future costs expected to triple, quadruple, quintuple. The expressway was renamed W. R. Allen Road. From Lawrence south to Eglinton, it had remained unbuilt. Uptown wags called it the Davis Ditch, the road to nowhere. Your favourite part came next: newspaper photos of kids on their bikes, wheelies on the unpaved roadbed. Such whimsy. In the distance, not even a speck of

Chevies or Cadillacs. You wish it ended there. GO mouthpiece Esther Shiner, elected to North York council in 1973, insisted that this unfinished stretch be completed. The province said no. The city said no. Metro said yes. So, in 1976, we were all nudged one stop further. Cars quickly snarled in every direction. Pedestrian crossings were placed, with impressive counterintuition, at the exact point where drivers accelerated onto the ramps. It was the worst intersection in town. But Premier Davis was not outdone: he used his last day in office to extend his middle finger and lease one metre of land to the City of Toronto. The land, just beyond the Eglinton exit, blocks all possible construction. The lease was for ninety-nine years. See you in 2084.

◊

You don't bother to lock your bike. You remove your helmet. There's a crack in the shell. Deviant but unbroken, like a fracture in the skull. Your apartment is on the second floor of a semi-detatched. You drop your keys. Pick them up. Turn the lock. On the landing, Es waits. She has one hand on the banister, the other on her belly.

It's time, she says.

Notes and Acknowledgements

The history of the Spadina Expressway was much longer and more complicated than portrayed here. I have simplified events for the purposes of narrative.

Several books have informed this one, in ways both obvious and subtle:

All That Is Solid Melts into Air: The Experience of Modernity, by Marshall Berman; *The City in History: Its Origins, Its Transformations, and Its Prospects*, by Lewis Mumford; *The Bad Trip: The Untold Story of the Spadina Expressway*, by David and Nadine Nowlan; *The Uses of Disorder: Personal Identity and City Life*, by Richard Sennett.

Quotations and references are from, in order of appearance:

p. 16, 'My nerves are strained...': Yevgeny Yevtushenko, *Bratsk Station and Other New Poems*, 1967

p. 28, '...more wildness in thinking than in lust': Leonard Michaels, *Shuffle*, 1990

p. 36: '...in the instant of becoming': William James, *The Principles of Pyschology*, Vol. 1, 1890

p. 112: 'The apartment is quiet as paper': Nadezhda Mandelstam, quoting the first line of a poem by her husband, Osip Mandelstam, *Hope Against Hope: A Memoir*, 1970

p. 117: 'But if we are building a transportation system...':
William B. Davis, speaking to the Legislative Assembly of
Ontario, June 3, 1971.

Financial assistance from the following is much appreciated:
Toronto Arts Council, Ontario Arts Council, the Canada
Council for the Arts, and, most importantly, the Writers'
Trust of Canada's Woodcock Fund.

Thank you to my regular trio of readers: Jason McBride,
Derek McCormack, and Adam Sternbergh.

Special thanks to John Fraser.

Deep gratitude to everyone at Coach House Books, especially Alana Wilcox.

And, as always, to Suse.

Howard Akler is the author of two books with Coach House: *The City Man*, which was nominated for the Amazon First Novel Award, the City of Toronto Book Award, and the Commonwealth Writers Prize, and *Men of Action*, which won the Canadian Jewish Literary Award for Memoir, was shortlisted for the Toronto Book Award, and was featured as a part of the 2015 *New York Times* Gift Guide.

Typeset in Albertan, Tape Type, and Squareface

Albertan was designed by the late Jim Rimmer of New Westminster, B.C.,
in 1982. He drew and cut the type in metal at the 16-pt size in roman only;
it was intended for use only at his Pie Tree Press. He drew the italic in
1985, designing it with a narrow fit and a very slight incline, and created a
digital version. The family was completed in 2005, when Rimmer redrew
the bold weight and called it Albertan Black. The letterforms of this type
family have an old-style character, with Rimmer's own calligraphic hand
in evidence, especially in the italic.

Printed at the Coach House on bpNichol Lane in Toronto, Ontario, on
Zephyr Antique Laid paper, which was manufactured, acid-free, in Saint-
Jérôme, Quebec, from second-growth forests. This book was printed with
vegetable-based ink on a 1973 Heidelberg KORD offset litho press. Its
pages were folded on a Baumfolder, gathered by hand, bound on a Sulby
Auto-Minabinda, and trimmed on a Polar single-knife cutter.

Edited and designed by Alana Wilcox
Cover by Ingrid Paulson
Cover photograph from the City of Toronto Archives, Fonds 1567, Series
    648, File 246, Item 5

Coach House Books
80 bpNichol Lane
Toronto ON M5S 3J4
Canada

416 979 2217
800 367 6360

mail@chbooks.com
www.chbooks.com